# A WANDERER PLAYS
# ON MUTED STRINGS

CURRENT AMERICAN EDITIONS
OF WORKS BY KNUT HAMSUN

*Dreamers* (New York: New Directions)
*Growth of the Soil* (New York: Random House)
*Hunger* (New York: Farrar, Straus and Giroux)
*Hunger* (New York: PenguinPutnam)
*On Overgrown Paths*
(København and Los Angeles: Green Integer)
*Pan* (New York: Farrar, Straus and Giroux)
*Pan* (New York: PenguinPutnam)
*Rosa* (Los Angeles: Sun & Moon Press)
*Under the Autumn Star* (Los Angeles: Sun & Moon Press)
*Victoria* (Los Angeles: Sun & Moon Press)
*Wayfarers* (Los Angeles: Sun & Moon Press)
*The Women at the Pump* (Los Angeles: Sun & Moon Press)
*A Wanderer Plays on Muted Strings*
(København and Los Angeles: Green Integer)


*Forthcoming*

*The Last Joy* (København and Los Angeles: Green Integer)

KNUT HAMSUN

# *A WANDERER PLAYS*
# *ON MUTED STRINGS*

\*

*Translated from the Norwegian*
*by Oliver and Gunnvor Stallybrass*

GREEN INTEGER
KØBENHAVEN & LOS ANGELES
2001

GREEN INTEGER
Edited by Per Bregne
København/Los Angeles

Distributed in the United States by Consortium Book
Sales and Distribution, 1045 Westgate Drive, Suite 90
Saint Paul, Minnesota 55114-1065

(323) 857-1115 / http://www.greeninteger.com

10 9 8 7 6 5 4 3 2 1

Design: Per Bregne
Typography: Guy Bennett
Photograph: Photograph of Knut Hamsun

LIBRARY OF CONGRESS CATALOGING IN PUBLICATION DATA
Hamsun, Knut [1859–1952]
*A Wanderer Plays on Muted Strings*
ISBN 1-892295-73-3
p. cm — Green Integer: 13
I. Title II. Series III. Translation: Oliver and Gunnvor Stallybrass

It looked like being a good year for berries: red whortleberries, crowberries, and cloudberries. Not that one can live on berries. But it is good that they should grow there in the meadows and be so inviting to the eye. And they are refreshing things to find when you are thirsty and hungry.

Such had been my thoughts the night before.

I knew, of course, that it was several months before the late autumn berries would be ripe. But the woods and the fields give other joys than berries. In spring and summer the berries are mere blossoms as yet; but there are bluebells and babies' slippers, deep windless forests, the scent of trees, stillness. The roar of a distant torrent descends on the ear as if from heaven—the most long-drawn-out sound in time or eternity. And if a song thrush sings so that his voice soars God-how-high, and if while poised up there on the topmost note he suddenly makes a right angle in the pitch, the line as clear and as clean as if cut with a diamond; then he sings down the scale again, softly and beautifully. Along the shore, too, there is life: guillemots and oyster catchers and terns are running about; the wagtail is out finding food, moving in little spurts, bobbing his tail, sharp beaked and elegant; then he flies up on a fence, and he too sings. But when the sun has gone down, then sometimes a grebe strikes up his melancholy *hurra* from a remote mountain lake. He is the last. Now there is only the grasshopper, about whom there is nothing to say, he is so invisible and insignificant. He lies there, as if rubbing himself in resin.

All this I had sat and pondered: how summer too had its joys for the wanderer, so there was no need to wait until the fall.

Now, however, I reflect on how I sit writing calm words about these peaceful things—for all the world as if I were not coming, later, to violent and dangerous events. It is just a trick I learned from a man in the Southern Hemisphere, from Rough, a Mexican. Brass spangles tinkled around the brim of his enormous hat; that alone brings him vividly to mind. But I remember, above all, how calmly he spoke of his first murder. "I once had a sweetheart called Maria," Rough recalled with his air of resignation. "Come to think of it, she was only sixteen at the time, and I was nineteen. Her hands were so tiny that when it came to thanking me for something or saying hello, all you could feel were her bony fingers; that's the kind she was. One evening the boss called her in from the fields to do some sewing for him. There was nothing to stop him, and a day or two later he called her in again from the fields to sew. It went on like this for several weeks, then it stopped. Seven months later Maria died and was buried in the ground, tiny hands and all. I went to her brother Inez and said, 'At six o'clock tomorrow morning the boss is riding into town, and he'll be alone.' 'I know,' he said. 'You might lend me that little rifle of yours to shoot him with tomorrow,' I said. 'I shall be using it myself,' he said. So we talked for a bit about other things, about the harvest and about a big well we'd dug; when I left I took down his rifle from the wall and took it with me. In the forest Inez was at my heels and shouted to me to stop. We sat down and talked some more about this and that, and after a bit Inez snatched the rifle from me and went back home. Early next morning I was waiting by the gate to open it for the boss, and Inez was there too, in the bushes. I said to him, 'You'd better start walking on ahead, so we're not two against one.' 'He's got pistols in his belt,' said Inez; 'what have you got?' 'I've got nothing like that,' I said, 'but I've got a lump of lead in my hand, and that makes no noise.' Inez had a look at the lead and thought for a bit; then he nodded and went home. Then the boss came riding up; he was old and gray, sixty at least. 'Open the gate!' he shouted. But I never

7

opened the gate. I suppose he thought I'd gone mad. He cracked his whip at me, but I took no notice. So he had to get off himself and open the gate. Then I gave him the first blow, it got him in the eye and cracked a hole open. 'Ah-ur-gh!' he said and went sprawling. I said a few words to him, but he didn't understand, and after a few more blows he was dead. He had stacks of money in his pocket, I took what I needed for the journey, then I mounted and rode off. Inez was standing by the door as I passed. 'You can make the border in three and a half days,' he said."

That was how Rough told his story, gazing calmly in front of him when he had finished.

I have no murders to tell about, but I have joys and sufferings and love. And love is every bit as violent and dangerous as murder.

It is green now in every wood, I thought to myself that morning as I dressed. The snow is melting on the mountains, everywhere now the cattle are standing in the barns, chafing to be let out, and in human habitations windows are thrown wide open. I unbuttoned my shirt, let the wind blow in on me, and became a star-struck, seething mass of unruliness within—ah, for a moment I was back in old times, when I was younger and more tempestuous than I am now. If there should chance to be a forest east or west of here, I thought, where an old man can thrive as well as a young, that is where I shall go!

Rain and sun and wind in alternation. I had already been walking for many days; it was still too cold to sleep out at night, but I had no trouble finding shelter on the farms. One man marveled at my walking and walking without apparent purpose. I must be someone in disguise, acting the eccentric—a poet, perhaps. The man knew nothing of my plans: that I was en route for familiar places where lived certain people I wanted to see again. But his intellect was good, and I involuntarily nodded, as if to say there was something in what he said. There's a large theatrical element in all of us; we feel flattered at being taken for more than we are. But then his wife and daughter joined in, maundering away at us in their everyday language of the heart: "But he hasn't been begging at all," they said; "he paid for his evening meal!" Now I turned cowardly and crafty to the core, said nothing to this, and allowed the man to make further accusations, to which likewise I offered no reply. And we three people of the heart defeated the man with his intellect: he had to explain that he was joking, surely we were capable of seeing a joke! I stayed on this farm for a night and a day, greasing my shoes with special care and mending my clothes.

But then the man became suspicious of me again. "When you leave you'll be giving my daughter a handsome tip," he said. I affected nonchalance and answered with a laugh, "Will I really?"

"Yes," he replied, "and then we'll sit back and think what a very superior person you must have been."

How unspeakably offensive he was! I did the only thing possible: ignored his taunts, and asked for work. I liked it here, I said; he could do with my help for the season, I could turn my hand to anything he cared to mention. "I'd rather see you clear right off," the man retorted; "you fool, you!"

It was clear that he had made me the object of his hatred; and none of the womenfolk were at hand to take my part. I looked at him, unable to make him out. His gaze was steady, and suddenly it seemed to me that I had never seen such intelligent eyes in anyone. But he carried his malignity too far and went off the rails. "What shall we say your name was?" he asked. "You don't need to say it was anything," I answered. "A wandering John Wesley?" he hazarded. I entered into the joke and said, "Yes, why not?" But this answer acted on the man like a goad; he became more and more saucy and said, "I feel sorry for Mrs. Wesley, then!" At which I shrugged my shoulders and replied, "You're mistaken; I'm not married." And with that I turned to go. But with unnatural quickness of wit he shouted after me, "It's you who's mistaken: I was referring to the mother who bore you!"

Down in the road, I turned and saw that the man had been taken in hand by his wife and daughter. And I thought to myself: No, it's not exactly roses, roses all the way when you go wandering.

At the next farm I learned that the man was a former quartermaster sergeant; then for a time he had been in a lunatic asylum, through losing a case in the Supreme Court. This spring his illness had broken out again; perhaps it was my coming that had given him the final push over the edge. But the lightning flashes of insight he had shown at the very moment when the madness closed over him! I remember him from time to time, and he certainly taught me a lesson: how hard it is to judge people correctly, who is mad and who is wise. And may God preserve us all from being seen through!

That day I came past a house where a youngster sat on the doorstep playing a mouth organ. He was no great performer, but he must have been a happy soul to sit there playing to himself. I just touched my cap so as not to disturb him, and remained standing at a distance. He took no notice of me; instead, he wiped his mouth organ dry, put it to his mouth, and started playing again. This went on for some time, until I took advantage of another wiping session and coughed. "Is that you Ingeborg?" he asked. I thought he was talking over his shoulder to some woman in the house and made no answer. "You standing there," he said. I asked in some confusion, "Me? Can't you see me?" To this he made no reply, but fumbled a little all around him, as if to get up. Then I realized he was blind. "Sit still, don't let me frighten you," I said, and sat down beside him.

We chatted about one thing and another; he was about eighteen, blind from his fourteenth year, tall and strong, the lower half of his face downy with an incipient beard. Thank God, he said, his health was good. But his eyesight, I said—did he still remember what the world looked like? Oh yes, he had many nice memories from the time when he saw. All in all, he was contented and happy. He was going to Christiania this spring, to a professor who would operate on him and perhaps even give him back part of his sight! Ah yes, one day all would be well! His wits were limited, he looked like a heavy eater: stout, and strong as a beast. But there was something unhealthy-looking about him, something of the idiot; his devotion to his destiny was more than a little foolish. Surely such optimism argued stupidity; there must be a certain lack of gray matter in a man who could go around in permanent contentment with life, and even expect something new and good from it.

But I was in the mood to learn something from all I met on my wanderings; even this poor lad who sat here on his doorstep had made me wiser in one small respect. How had he managed to mistake me for the woman called Ingeborg, whose name he had called? I must have been walking too quietly, I had forgotten my cart-horse role, my shoes were too light. I had been corrupted by the refinements of many years, I must take a refresher course in being a peasant.

Three more days now to the goal which my curiosity had set itself: to Øvrebø, to Captain Falkenberg's place. It made excellent sense to arrive there on foot just now and ask for work: in the long spring season there was plenty to do on such a large estate. It was six years since I had been there last; the time had gone by, and for several weeks I had let my beard grow, so that no one would recognize me.

It was now midweek; I must arrange things so that I arrived on Saturday evening. Then the Captain would let me stay there over Sunday while he considered my request, and on Monday he would come and say yes or no.

Strangely enough, I felt no excitement, no unrest,

at the thought of what was looming up ahead; at a good, leisurely pace I came wandering past farms and woods and meadows. I thought to myself: And yet this same Øvrebø was once the scene of some eventful weeks in my life; I was even in love with Madame, with the Captain's wife, Louise. Most certainly I was. She had fair hair and dark-gray eyes, and she was like a young girl. It was six years ago, an eternity ago; would she be greatly changed? For myself, time had made heavy inroads on me, I had grown dull and withered and indifferent—I looked at a woman now the way I looked at literature. The end had come. So what? Everything must have an end. In the early stages of this condition I felt as if I had lost something, as if some benevolent pickpocket had been at work. Then I set myself to find out whether I could endure my own company any longer, whether I could put up with myself. Oh yes. Nothing was the same as before, but it had all happened silently, peacefully, inevitably. Everything must have an end.

In old age we no longer live our lives; we merely keep on our feet with the aid of memories. We are like a batch of letters that someone has sent: we are no longer in the post, we have arrived. The same is true whether our contents have stirred up joys and sorrows or whether they have made no impression at all. Thank you for life, it was fun to live!

As for woman, she was what all wise men have always known her to be: a pauper in talents, but rich in irresponsibility, in vanity, in wantonness; with much of the child but nothing of its innocence.

I stood by the signpost where the side road leads up to Øvrebø. I felt no emotion. The day lay broad and bright over meadows and woods, here and there the fields were being plowed and harrowed, but it was high noon and hot sun, and progress was so slow as to be almost imperceptible. I continued past the sign post, to fill in time before arriving at the manor. After an hour or so I turned off into the forest and wandered around for a while, amid the berry blossoms and the scent of small green leaves. Scores of thrushes were chasing a crow before them across the sky, kicking up an unholy din, like a babel of faulty castanets. I lay down on my back, with my sack under my head, and fell asleep.

On waking, I walked over to the nearest plowman, to make a few inquiries about the Falkenbergs of Øvrebø, whether they were still alive, whether they were flourishing. The man I encountered gave me cautious answers, standing there with his small, cunning eyes and saying, "Depends whether the Captain's at home." "Is he often away?" "No, he's at home, like as not." "Has he finished his plowing and sowing?" The man smiled. "No, I wouldn't say that." "Has he enough help?" "That I can't tell you—yes, belike he has. And the plowing and sowing's done—leastways, the manure's been carted out. Oh ay."

Then the man geed to his horses and continued plowing, while I walked beside him. There was not much to be learned from this man. The next time the horses stopped for a breather, I wormed out of him a few more contradictions about the people at Øvrebø. The Captain was with his regiment right through every summer, see, and then his lady was on her own. Oh yes, they always had lots of visitors, needless to say; but the Captain was away. That's to say, he liked it best at home, see, but he had to be with his regiment too. No; no children as yet, didn't look like she'd have any children, the lady, that was. "What am I saying, she could have lots of children yet, dozens of children, for that matter. Gee up!"

We plowed and paused for another breather. Not wanting to arrive at Øvrebø at an awkward moment, I asked the man if he thought they had company at the Captain's today. He thought not. Mind you, they often had company, but. And there was music and games and guests there all the time nowadays, but. That's to say, they were gentry, up at the Captain's, and they could afford it, no doubt, with all their riches and finery.

That plowman was a real pill. I tried, next, to find out something about another Falkenberg: Lars Falkenberg, my former mate in the timber felling, he who tuned pianos in a pinch. And now the man's information became much more definite: Lars? Sure, he was here. Should just think he did know Lars! He had finished working for the Captain, but the Captain had given him a small clearing to build on and live on; he had married Emma, one of the maids, and had two children. Good, hard-working people, who already had two cows on their clearing.

Here he reached the end of his furrow and turned the horses around, so I said goodbye and went.

As I stood in the courtyard at Øvrebø, I recognized all the buildings; but they needed painting. I noticed that the flagpole which I had helped to raise six years ago was still standing; but there was no halyard, and the knob at the top was missing.

I had arrived. It was four o'clock on the afternoon of the twenty-sixth of April.

Old people remember dates.

# I

It turned out differently from what I had imagined. Captain Falkenberg came out, heard my request, and turned it down then and there. He had all the help he needed, and the plowing and sowing were almost finished.

All right. Might I sit in the servants' hall and rest for a while?

By all means.

Without inviting me to stay over Sunday, the Captain turned on his heel and went back into the house. It seemed I had got him out of bed: he was still in his nightshirt and had no waistcoat on, having merely thrown on a jacket without buttoning it up. He had gone gray around the temples, and his beard was grizzled.

I sat in the servants' hall and waited for the farm-hands to come in for their afternoon meal. There was only a man and a boy, and when I got talking to them, it appeared to be a misunderstanding on the Captain's part about the plowing and sowing being almost finished. Ah well, that was his pigeon! I made no secret of the fact that I was looking for work; as for my capabilities, I let them read the excellent testimonial given me by the Sheriff at Hersæt in the old days. When it was time for the men to go, I shouldered my sack and went out with them, ready to leave. I had a quick look in at the stables (where there were a surprising number of horses), the barn, the poultry, and the pigs; in the bin I saw manure from last year which had not yet been carted out.

"How can that be?"

"Well, what can one do?" answered the older of the hands. "I was carting manure from late winter onward, all on my own. Now there are two of us, after a fashion, but there's the plowing and harrowing to do."

His pigeon!

"Well, goodbye," I said, and went. I intended to call on my good comrade Lars Falkenberg, but this I kept quiet about. I had glimpsed a cluster of small new buildings far up in the forest and reckoned that must be Lars's place.

The foreman must have been inwardly grieved at the loss to Øvrebø of a man to help with the seasonal work; as I set off I saw him tramp across the yard and enter the house.

I had gone a hundred yards or so when the foreman came running after me with the news that I had been taken on after all; he had spoken with the Captain and been given a free hand to employ me. "There's nothing for you to do until Monday; but come in and have some food!"

The foreman was a good, straightforward fellow; he came with me into the kitchen to break the news. "Give this man something to eat—he's going to work here!"

New cook, new maids. I had my meal and went out again. No sign of the master or the mistress.

I got bored with sitting idle in the servants' room all evening, so I followed the farmhands out into the field and chatted with them. The foreman came from a farm a little to the north, but since he wasn't the oldest son and had no farm of his own to manage, he had made up his mind to serve at Øvrebø for a time. And indeed he could have done a lot worse. The Captain concerned himself steadily less and less with the estate—not to mention his long absences; so the foreman had often to use his own judgment. Last autumn he had turned over large expanses of marshy land which he intended to sow. And he pointed with his finger. Here he had plowed, here he would let well enough alone; look at that field he'd reclaimed last year, wasn't it a lovely sight already?

It was good to hear how well the young man knew his job, and his sensible talk put me in good heart. He had also attended the county high school, where he had learned to keep farming accounts, entering hayloads in one column and calves' birthdays in another. His pigeon! In earlier days a peasant kept such accounts in his head, and his womenfolk knew to the day when each and every one of their twenty or fifty cows was due to calve.

But the foreman had his wits about him, nevertheless, and was not afraid of hard work—though recently he had been somewhat overwhelmed by the sheer insuperable volume of work on the Captain's estate. It was an obvious encouragement that now he was getting an extra pair of hands. Starting on Monday, he decided, I was to take the horse from the harrowing and use it to cart manure, while the boy used one of the Captain's two carriage horses for the harrowing; the foreman himself would stick to the plowing. Ah yes, we would get this year's seed sown yet!

Sunday.

I had to be careful not to know anything from my previous stay here: for example, how far the Captain's woods stretched, where the various buildings and outbuildings were situated, or the well, or the roads. I busied myself getting ready for the morning, greasing the cart and the harness, giving my horse a little extra attention. After dinner I spent four or five hours wandering around in the Captain's woods, passed Lars's cottage without going in, and went as far as the parish boundary before turning back. I was amazed to see how many trees had been felled.

When I got back the foreman asked, "Did you hear the singing and carrying on last night?"

"Yes. Who was it?"

"The visitors." He laughed.

The visitors, to be sure. The place was always full of them these days.

They included an exceedingly fat but lively gentleman with a cavalry mustache who was a captain in the same regiment as Captain Falkenberg; in the course of the evening I saw him and the other guests come trickling out of the house. There was also a man they addressed as Engineer; he was young, early twenties, medium height, dark-complexioned, and clean-shaven. And there was Elizabeth from the parsonage. I had vivid memories of Elizabeth, so I had no difficulty in recognizing her now, even though she was six years older and more mature. Little Elizabeth of the old days was no longer a girl; her breast stood out strongly and gave an impression of exaggeratedly good health. The foreman told me she had married: she had accepted young Eric after all—a young farmer's son she had been fond of since childhood days. She was still friendly with Mrs. Falkenberg and a frequent visitor at Øvrebø. But her husband never came with her.

And now Captain Falkenberg came and joined Elizabeth, who was standing by the flagpole. They chatted away, engrossed in their conversation; the Captain glanced around him each time before he spoke, so perhaps it was not trivialities he was talking but some topic demanding caution.

Next came the fat, jolly captain; his laughter reached us over in the servants' hall. He called to Falkenberg to join him but received only a short answer, delivered slantwise. There were some stone steps leading down to a lilac grove; and there the fat captain proceeded, followed by a maid with wine and glasses, and the engineer bringing up the rear.

The foreman burst out laughing and said, "Really, that captain!"

"What's his name?"

"They all just call him Brother; they called him that last year too. I don't know what his real name is."

"And the engineer?"

"His name's Lassen, I believe. He's been here only once before in my time."

Then Mrs. Falkenberg came out onto the front steps; she stopped for a moment and stood looking at the couple over by the flagpole. Her figure was still neat and elegant, but her features were sagging; her cheeks seemed to have shrunk, compared with her former fullness. She too made her way to the lilac grove, and I recognized her walk, which was as easy and supple as ever. It was only to be expected that after all these years she should have lost much of her good looks.

More people came out from the house: a middle-aged lady with a shawl around her, accompanied by two gentlemen.

The foreman told me there were not always quite so many visitors about the place; but two days ago it had been the Captain's birthday, when two carriage-loads of people had come dashing up; the four strange horses were in the stable yet.

And now they were shouting in earnest for the two by the flagpole. "Coming!" called the Captain impatiently; but he still lingered on. Now he was flicking a speck of dust from Elizabeth's shoulder, now he was having a good look around before laying a hand on her arm as he impressed some point upon her.

The foreman said, "They always have so much to talk about, those two. She never comes here without their taking long walks together."

"Doesn't Mrs. Falkenberg mind?"

"Not that I know of."

"And hasn't Elizabeth got any children either?"

"Oh yes, she's got several."

"How does she manage to get away so often from her children and that big farm?"

"As long as Eric's mother's alive there's no problem; she can easily get away."

The foreman went out, leaving me alone in the servants' hall. Here I had sat, once upon a time, constructing a remarkable felling saw. How absorbed in it I had been! One of the farmhands, Peter, lay sick in the little adjoining bedroom; but I was agog with eagerness and would run out into the passage whenever I wanted to chop or hammer. Now I thought of that felling saw the way I thought about literature. That is what time does to us all.

The foreman came in again.

"If the visitors are still here tomorrow, I'm taking two of their horses for plowing with," he said, engrossed in his own concerns.

I looked out of the window. The couple by the flagpole had moved away at last.

As the evening went on, things became more and more lively down in the lilac grove; the maids went to and fro carrying trays of food as well as of drink, for the gentry were having supper under the bushes. Suddenly there were shouts of "Brother! Brother!" with Brother himself laughing and shouting louder than anyone. His chair had broken under that enormous weight; and now came a request to the servants' hall for a really good, solid, wooden chair capable of supporting him. Oh yes, they were enjoying themselves down in the grove all right. From time to time Captain Falkenberg came up to the courtyard to show that he could still walk straight and was thoroughly in command of the situation.

"I put my money on him," said the foreman. "He's not the man to pack it in first. Once last year, when I was driving him, he never stopped drinking the whole way, but it didn't make the slightest difference to him."

The sun went down. It must have turned chilly in the grove, because the gentry moved indoors. But the great living-room windows were thrown wide open, and waves of melodious sound from Mrs. Falkenberg's piano surged out to us. Later on there was dance music—played, I guess, by fat Captain Brother.

"What a crew!" the foreman muttered. "Dancing and playing all night, sleeping all day. I'm turning in now."

I remained sitting by the window, and saw my old comrade Lars Falkenberg cross the yard and enter the house; he had been sent for to sing to the gentry. After a while, Captain Brother and a few more started helping out with their voices, until the rafters fairly rang with the merriment. In an hour or so Lars Falkenberg came to the servants' hall, in his pocket a half bottle they had given him for his pains. Finding only me, a stranger, in the hall, he went into the bedroom and had a drop or two with the foreman; after a while I was invited to join them. I took care not to say too much and so give myself away; but when Lars left to go home he asked me to accompany him for part of the way. Then it appeared that I had already been seen through; that Lars knew I was his mate from the timber-felling days.

The Captain had told him.

Good, I thought: in that case there was no point in my taking further precautions. In short, I was far from displeased at this turn of events: it meant the Captain was supremely indifferent to my sauntering about the place as I pleased.

I walked all the way home with Lars Falkenberg, chatting with him about the old days, about his clearing, and about the people down on the manor. The Captain was no longer held in the same high regard; he had ceased to be the spokesman for the district, and people no longer came as they used to, both men and women, to seek his advice. Take the drive down to the main road: rebuilding that had been the last thing he did—and that was five years ago. The buildings needed painting, but he let them be. The farmland had been misused, the woods too heavily plundered. Did he drink? Well, so it was said, but it wasn't strictly true—devil take all gossips and slanderers! He drank a little; and apart from that he would drive off from time to time and stay away for a while; but when he did come home again, he had no go in him then either—that was the tragedy. It was as if an evil spirit had got into him, said Lars.

And Madame?

Madame! She went around as before, playing her piano and looking as pretty as a picture. "And they keep open house, with visitors all the time. But they pay heavy taxes of one kind and another, and it costs a mint just to keep all those great buildings. But it's a real judgment on the pair of them how dead weary they are of each other—you wouldn't believe it. If they do ever say a word to each other, they look some other way and hardly open their lips. They don't speak for anyone to notice, except to other people, for months on end. And in the summer the Captain's with his regiment and never comes home or gives a thought to his wife or the place. Ah, but they've no children—that's the trouble!" said Lars.

Emma came out from the cottage and joined us. She looked extremely well and as pretty as ever, and I told her so. "Oh, Emma's well enough," Lars agreed; "but she never stops having children, the monster!" With which he handed her his half bottle and forced her to drink what was left. Emma wanted us all to go in. "We might just as well be sitting in comfort indoors as standing here." "Ah, but it's summertime now," replied Lars, who was by no means anxious to invite me in. When I left, he came with me again for a little way, pointing out to me where he had dug and ditched and fenced on his little clearing. He had made a good, intelligent job of his miniature farm, and I was filled with a strange delight as I stood outside this snug little home in the forest. Behind the cottage and the barn the wind soughed gently through the pine forest; beside them grew deciduous trees, with aspen leaves rustling like silk.

I walked home. The evening wore on, the birds were all silent, the air mild, the twilight soft and blue.

"Let us be young tonight!" came loud and clear in a man's voice from behind the lilacs. "Let us dance in the calf pen tonight!"

"Do you remember what you were like last year?" came Mrs. Falkenberg's voice in reply. "You were young and sweet then, and didn't say such things."

"No, then I didn't say such things. To think that you still remember! But last year too you scolded me one night. 'You're very beautiful tonight,' I said. 'No,' you answered, 'I'm not beautiful any more; and you're a child, and you mustn't drink so much," you said.

"Yes, that's what I said," answered Mrs. Falkenberg with a laugh.

"Yes, that's what you said. But surely I ought to have known whether you were beautiful, since I was sitting there looking at you."

"You child, you child!"

"And tonight you're even more beautiful."

"There's someone coming."

Two figures stood erect behind the lilacs: Mrs. Falkenberg and the visiting engineer. When they saw it was only me, they breathed more easily again and went on talking as if I didn't exist. And—such is human nature—although I had only wanted to be left in peace by everyone, yet now I was offended because these two held me in such small esteem. What if my hair and beard are gray, I asked myself; should they not honor me therefore?

"Yes, and tonight you're even more beautiful," repeated the engineer.

I walked right past them, touched my cap casually, and continued on my way.

"All I can say is that it won't do you any good," answered Madame. "You've lost something!" she called after me.

Lost? My handkerchief lay on the path, where I had deliberately dropped it; now I turned and picked it up, murmured some thanks, and went on my way again.

"What a sharp eye you've got for irrelevant objects!" said the engineer. "A peasant's rag with red flowers on it! Come, let's go into the summerhouse!"

"It's locked at night," answered Madame. "Perhaps there's someone in there."

After that I heard no more.

My sleeping quarters were in the loft over the servants' hall, and I had left open a window facing the grove. When I came up there, I could still hear voices behind the bushes, but not the actual words. I thought to myself: Why is the summerhouse locked at night, and whose idea was that? Perhaps some crafty character's who thought that if this door was always kept locked, it would be less risky to slip away one night in good company, take the key, and stay there.

Some distance down the path I had just taken I saw two people approaching: the fat Captain Brother and the middle-aged lady with the shawl. They must have been sitting somewhere in the grove as I passed; and now I began to wonder whether I might have been talking aloud to myself and said anything in their hearing.

Suddenly I saw the engineer get up from behind the bushes and hurry across to the summerhouse. Finding the door locked, he put his shoulder to it and broke it open. There was a splintering sound.

"Come on, there's no one here!" he called.

Mrs. Falkenberg stood up and said in great indignation, "What are you up to, you madman?"

However, even as she spoke, she was moving toward him.

"Up to?" he answered. "Love isn't glycerine, it's nitroglycerine. "

Then he took Mrs. Falkenberg by the arm and led her in.

Their pigeon.

But now the fat captain and his lady came strolling along—quite unbeknownst, probably, to the pair in the summerhouse. Mrs. Falkenberg would hardly be best pleased at being discovered alone with a man in such a secluded spot. I looked around my room for some means of warning them, and found an empty bottle; I positioned myself by the window and hurled it with all my strength toward the summerhouse. There was a crash of breaking glass and tiles, followed by the clatter of fragments down the roof; at the same moment there was a cry of terror from the summerhouse, and Mrs. Falkenberg came storming out, followed by the engineer, who still had hold of her clothes. They stopped for a moment to peer around. "Brother! Brother!" exclaimed Mrs. Falkenberg, and sped away down through the grove. "No, don't come with me!" she called back over her shoulder, "you're *not* to come with me."

Undeterred, the engineer ran in pursuit. He was marvelously young and utterly relentless.

But now came the fat captain and his lady, conducting a priceless conversation, as if it was only love that made the world go round. The fat gentleman must have been close on sixty, the woman he was with around forty; their tender affection was a sight for sore eyes.

The fat captain said, "Until tonight it has been just within the bounds of endurance; but now it taxes a man beyond his strength—Madame, you have utterly bewitched me."

"I didn't realize it was so serious," she answered, speaking kindly to him and helping him along.

"But it is," he retorted. "And now I must put an end to it, I tell you. We have just come from the grove; there I thought I could bear it for one more night, so I didn't say much. But now I beg you to come back to the grove with me."

She shook her head.

"No; I do so much want to be your...do what you—"

*"Thank* you!" he exclaimed.

And he threw his arms around her in the middle of the path, and pressed his round belly against hers. They looked like two refractory combatants. That scamp of a captain!

"Let me go!" she begged.

He relaxed his grip a little, then tightened it again. And again it looked as if they were locked in combat.

"Come back with me to the grove!" he said again and again.

"Out of the question," she answered. "Especially now, with all this dew."

But the captain was full of amorous words, and now he let them overflow.

"Ah, time was I harbored churlish thoughts about eyes. Blue eyes—bah! Gray eyes—bah! A gaze of any color, be it ever so intense—again and yet again, bah! But then came you with your brown eyes!"

"Yes, they are brown," the lady conceded.

"You are burning me with them, you are roasting me the same color."

"In fact, you're not the first person to praise my eyes. My husband—"

"But what about me?" cried the captain. "I tell you, purely and simply, that if I had met you twenty years ago, I would not have answered for my reason. Come with me now, there really isn't all that much dew in the grove."

"Let's go indoors, rather," she suggested.

"Indoors! There's not one single corner where we can be alone. "

"I think we'll find a place," she replied.

"Yes, because I must put an end to this tonight," said the captain.

And they went.

I asked myself: was it really to warn someone that I had thrown that empty bottle?


At three in the morning I heard the foreman go out and feed the horses. At four he knocked on the ceiling below where I slept. He was welcome to the privilege of being the first man astir, though I could have woken him at any hour of the night; for I had not slept. It was no great matter to go without sleep for a night or two in this fine, light air, which did not make for drowsiness.

The foreman set out for the fields, driving a new plow team. He had inspected the visiting horses and chosen Elizabeth's. They were good farm horses, with coarse legs.

## II

More visitors arrived at Øvrebø; the merriment never let up. Meanwhile, we farmhands manured and plowed and sowed. Some of the fields were already sprouting green in our wake—a sight which filled us with joy.

But from time to time we had to overcome opposition from Captain Falkenberg himself. "He's given up using his wits or caring about his interests," said the foreman. Yes, an evil spirit had indeed got into him: he went around half drunk, half listless, preoccupied with his role of incomparable host; for nearly a week now he had joined his guests in turning day into night and night into day. And the racket at night was such that the beasts in the stables and barns could get no rest; nor could the maids sleep at the proper time, for the young gentlemen even came into their quarters at night and sat on their beds chatting with them, for the pleasure of seeing them undressed.

We working folk took no part in this, of course; but many a time we felt more sad than proud to be serving on the Captain's estate. The foreman got hold of a temperance badge and wore it outside his smock.

One day the Captain came to me in the fields and ordered me to get out the carriage and fetch two new visitors from the station. It was mid-afternoon, and he had doubtless just got up. He had me in a tight spot; and why had he not gone to the foreman? Was he beginning to get embarrassed by that temperance badge? The Captain must have seen that I was hanging back; he smiled and said, "Afraid of what Nils might say? In that case I'd better speak to him first."

Nils was the name of the foreman.

But I just didn't dare let the Captain go over to Nils at that moment—he was still plowing with the visitors' horses and had asked me to tip him off if there was any danger of discovery. I took out my handkerchief, wiped my face, and waved a little; the foreman saw me and at once unhitched the horses from the plow. What will he do now? I wondered. Aha! The admirable Nils would manage all right: although it was much too early for knocking off, he started taking the horses home.

If only I could now delay the Captain a little! The foreman realized what was up: he pressed on, and he already, while still on the way home, started undoing the harness.

The Captain looked at me suddenly and said, "' you lost your tongue?"

"Nils seems to be in trouble of some kind," I said; "he's unhitched the horses."

"Well? And?"

"Well, I just thought…"

But to hell with standing there dissembling! I could help Nils a little now; the coming storm he would have to weather for himself. I went straight to the point and said, "Well, it's like this: it's the sowing season now, and over there it's already starting to grow where we've been; but we've still got a lot of ground to—"

"All right, let it grow, let it grow."

"There's three acres of arable here, and another three and a half where Nils is working, and I thought perhaps the Captain might reconsider his order."

The Captain turned on his heel and left me without more words.

I'll have to walk the plank, I thought. But I obeyed orders and followed him home with the horse and cart.

By now I felt easy about the foreman; he had almost reached the outbuildings. The Captain beckoned to him, but without avail. Then he called "Halt!" in his best officer's voice; but the foreman heard nothing.

By the time we reached the stables, the foreman had the horses back in their stalls. The Captain's manner was stiff in the extreme; but he had evidently been having second thoughts during his walk.

"Why have you brought the horses in?" he asked.

"The plow broke down," answered the foreman.

"I'm stabling the horses while I fix it—it won't take long."

The Captain gave his order: "One of you is to take the carriage to the station."

The foreman glanced at me and mumbled, "Hm. I see. But is this really the right time for it?"

"What's that you're muttering about?"

"We're two and a half men," answered the foreman, "for the entire spring work. It's none too many."

But the Captain must have become suspicious about those chestnuts that the foreman had driven home in such a hurry. He went up to each animal in turn, to find which were warm; then he drew himself up in front of us, wiped his hands with his handkerchief, and said, "Are you plowing with other people's horses, Nils?"

Pause.

"I won't have it."

"Hm. No, I see," answered the foreman. But suddenly he flared up and went on, "We've more need of horses at Øvrebø this spring than any previous spring, we're breaking more soil than ever before. And these visitors' horses stood here day after day, eating and eating, not even earning the water they drank. So I took them out for a little spell now and again and loosened up their joints for them."

40

The Captain repeated, speaking very clearly, "I won't have it any more. Do you hear, Nils?"

Pause.

"Didn't you say one of the Captain's plow horses was unwell yesterday?" I put in.

The foreman seized on this. "Yes, that's right. Stood shivering in its stall. So I couldn't take it out."

The Captain measured me from top to toe. Then he said, "What are you standing there for?"

"The Captain ordered me to drive to the station."

"Then go and get ready."

But Nils took him up on the instant.

"No, it's no use."

Bravo, Nils! I said to myself. He was absolutely right, and he looked it too, as he stuck firmly and steadfastly to his guns. As for the horses, our own animals had been worked to exhaustion during the long spring season, while the visitors' horses stood there doing nothing but eat, and spoiling for want of exercise.

"No use?" asked the Captain, thunderstruck.

"If the Captain takes away my help, then I've finished here," said Nils.

The Captain went to the stable door and stood there, staring ahead of him, biting his mustache, and thinking. Then he said over his shoulder, "Can't you spare the lad either?"

"No, he's on the harrowing."

It was the first time we had collided head-on with the Captain and come out best. Later we had a few small tussles, but he soon gave in.

"There's a crate to come up from the station," he said one day; "can the boy fetch it?"

"The boy's as valuable as a man to us at present; he's doing the harrowing. If he drives to the station now, he won't be back till tomorrow evening—that's a day and a half lost."

Bravo! I said to myself again. Nils had told me earlier about this crate at the station: it contained fresh supplies of liquor. The maids had heard about it.

They exchanged a few more words; the Captain wrinkled his brow and opined that never before had the spring season lasted so long. Finally the foreman said in exasperation, "If you take the boy away from the field, I quit!" Then he went further, as we had agreed beforehand, and asked me, "Do you quit too?"

"Yes," I replied.

At this the Captain yielded and said with a smile, "A conspiracy, I see. Still, I have to admit you're right in a way. And you have green thumbs."

But our green thumbs were something which the Captain was hardly qualified to judge, and which gave him little pleasure. He probably cast an eye over the fields from time to time and formed the impression that plenty of plowing and sowing had taken place, but that was all. As for us farmhands, we worked and worked, and served our master and mistress to the uttermost. That was our way.

That, I suppose, was our way.

And yet there were times when our immense zeal came under suspicion: was it, perhaps, not quite so exalted after all? The foreman was a local man who wanted to get through his season's work at least as quickly as other local men; his honor was at stake. And I shared his feeling. Then again, when the foreman took to wearing a temperance badge, his main motive may well have been to get the Captain sober enough to notice our splendid efforts. And in this respect too I felt as he did. Perhaps, moreover, I entertained the hope that Madame—well, that Mrs. Falkenberg should understand what good souls we were. I doubt if I was above such considerations.

The first time I saw Mrs. Falkenberg at close quarters was one afternoon when I was coming out of the kitchen and she was crossing the courtyard, slender and bareheaded. I raised my peaked cap and looked at her; her face was strangely young and innocent. With perfect indifference she answered, "Good day!" and walked past.

It could not be that everything was finished between the Captain and his wife. Or so I reasoned, on the strength of the following events:

Ragnhild, the parlormaid, was her mistress's friend and spy. She kept watch on her account, was last into bed, and stood on the stairs examining her hands and listening; if, when outside a door, she was suddenly called for, she would perform three or four silent leaps. She was an attractive girl, with particularly bright eyes, and, for good measure, admirably warm-blooded. One evening I caught her standing right outside the summerhouse, sniffing at the lilacs. She started at my coming, pointed warningly at the summerhouse, and ran off with her tongue between her teeth.

The Captain was well aware of Ragnhild's activities, and on one occasion said to his wife in everyone's hearing—he was drunk, no doubt, and irritated about something or other—"That Ragnhild's a devious creature. Can't think why we keep her on."

Madame answered, "It's not the first time you've wanted to get rid of Ragnhild; goodness only knows why—she's the best maid we've ever had."

"For a certain purpose, maybe" was the Captain's parting shot.

This gave me food for thought. Such might be Madame's cunning that she kept this spy merely to make it look as if she cared what the Captain got up to. The world would then conclude that Madame, poor thing, went around secretly longing for her husband, and being perpetually disappointed and wronged by him. And would she not then be fully justified in paying him back in his own coin? In heaven's name, might not this be the position?

But I was to change my opinion.

The following day the Captain altered his tactics. Having failed to get rid of Ragnhild, and of the vigilance she exercised when he lurked in some dark corner with Elizabeth or planned a late-evening tête-à-tête in the summerhouse, he now veered around and started paying court to the girl. Oho! That device was surely one which some woman, which Elizabeth, had helped him to hit on.

We farmhands were sitting at the long kitchen table; the maids were about their business, and Madame herself was there. Enter the Captain, with a brush in his hand.

"Give my coat a quick brush-down, will you?" he said to Ragnhild.

She did as she was asked. When she had finished, the Captain said, "Thank you, my dear!"

Madame looked a little surprised, and at once sent her maid on an errand up to the loft. The Captain watched her leave the room and said, "What wonderfully bright eyes that girl's got!"

I glanced across at Madame. Her eyes blazed, she flushed crimson, she moved toward the door. But then she turned, and now her face was pale. She had evidently made a quick decision. Speaking over her shoulder, she said to her husband, "I wonder if Ragnhild's eyes aren't just a shade too bright."

The Captain asked in surprise, "How so?"

Madame gave a little laugh, glanced toward where we sat at the table, and went on, "Well, she's started getting very friendly with the farmhands."

Silence in the kitchen.

"So perhaps it's best if she goes," said Madame.

There was a superb impudence in this performance of Madame's, but there was nothing we could do—we realized that she had simply used us as a stalking-horse.

As we left the kitchen, the foreman said indignantly, "I've a good mind to go in again and say a thing or two."

But it was not worth worrying about, and I dissuaded him.

Two or three days later, the Captain again found an opportunity to pay Ragnhild a crude compliment in his wife's hearing: "with a young body like yours" were the words in question.

Dear me, the conversational tone at Øvrebø nowadays! Every year it must have gone down and down, with drunken guests and idleness and indifference and childlessness all playing their part.

That evening Ragnhild came to me and told me she had been given notice. Madame hadn't bothered to give reasons, beyond making an insinuation about myself.

This, again, was disingenuous. Madame knew very well that I was not staying much longer in any case, so why make me a scapegoat? She wanted to put a spoke in her husband's wheel, that was the fact of the matter.

Ragnhild was duly distressed, and cried a little, and dabbed her eyes. But after a while she comforted herself with the notion that once I had gone Madame would withdraw her notice. Which I, in my heart of hearts, was convinced she would not do.

The Captain and Elizabeth might well be pleased: the tiresome parlormaid would soon be safely out of the way.

But how was one to know? There could easily be a mistake in my balance sheet of the situation. Certain new developments made me change my opinion once again. How hard it is to judge people correctly!

It became clear to me that Mrs. Falkenberg was really and truly jealous of her husband, not merely pretending jealousy in order to be free to go her own crooked ways. Not a bit of it. On the other hand, she could hardly have believed for one moment that her husband had his eye on the parlormaid. That was merely a trick and a pretense; she would use any and every means that suited her purpose. She had gone red in the kitchen, admittedly; but that was just a sudden, natural expression of injury over her husband's unseemly words, not real jealousy.

Her husband, however, was welcome to think she was jealous of the girl. That was precisely her intention. She was saying in plain language: "Yes, I am indeed jealous again; you see, all is as it used to be; I am yours for the taking!" Mrs. Falkenberg was better than I had thought. For years husband and wife had drifted further and further apart, indifferently, perhaps of late defiantly; now she wished to take the first step and show her love anew. That was it. But toward the one she feared most of all she would not show her jealousy for worlds: toward Elizabeth, that dangerous friend, so many years younger than herself.

That was it.

And the Captain? Did anything stir in him when he saw his wife turn red that day in the kitchen? Perhaps a faint memory of other days may possibly have flickered through his head, a sense of mild surprise, of gladness even. But not a trace of emotion did he show. Over the years his arrogance and defiance must have grown too strong. That was the way it looked.

But then came the developments I mentioned.

## III

Mrs. Falkenberg had for some time been playing a game with her husband. She had feigned indifference to his indifference, consoling herself now and then with flirtatious attentions from the guests in their house. Now these guests were leaving one by one. However, fat Captain Brother and the lady with the shawl remained; and so did the engineer, Lassen. Captain Falkenberg's reaction to this seemed to be: "By all means, my friend! Stay on for as long as you feel inclined!" Nor did he seem concerned by his wife's growing familiarity with the engineer, whom she had taken to calling Hugo, as he did. "Hugo!" she would call from the steps. And the Captain's voice would answer helpfully, "Hugo's gone down the drive!"

One day, however, I heard the Captain answer with a sarcastic smile and a gesture toward the lilac grove, "Little King Hugo is awaiting you in his kingdom." I saw Mrs. Falkenberg jump; then she gave an embarrassed laugh to cover her confusion and went down to join the engineer.

At last she had struck a spark from her husband. Now she would try to strike some more.

This was on a Sunday.

Later in the day Madame was unusually restless. She spoke a few words to me and commented on the good work that Nils and I had been doing.

"Lars has been to the post office for me today, to collect an important letter I'm expecting. Will you do me a service and go up to his cottage for it?"

I said I would do so with pleasure.

"Lars won't get back till about eleven o'clock this evening. So you don't need to go for a long time yet."

"Very good."

"And when you get back you're to give the letter to Ragnhild. "

This was the first time during my present stay at Øvrebø that Mrs. Falkenberg had spoken to me. The experience was so new that I went back to my bedroom and sat there, feeling like one restored to a semblance of life. One or two thoughts occurred to me also. It was sheer tomfoolery, I said to myself, pretending to be here incognito any longer—so why, in warm weather, be bothered with a long gray beard that made me look like a patriarch? I took a razor and shaved it right off.

Around ten o'clock I went up to the cottage. Lars was not yet back, and only arrived after I had been there a while with Emma. I took the letter and returned home. It was close on midnight.

Ragnhild was nowhere to be seen, and the other maids had gone to bed. I glanced at the lilac grove, where Captain Falkenberg and Elizabeth were sitting at the round stone table talking; they took no notice of me. Then I saw a light in Madame's room upstairs and had the inspired thought that tonight I looked as I had done six years ago, being clean-shaven now as then. I took the letter from my pocket and went in by the main door, to deliver the letter in person.

At the top of the stairs Ragnhild came bounding noiselessly up to me and took the letter. She was evidently in a state of intense excitement, and I felt the heat of her breath as she pointed across the landing— to where I could hear voices.

I got the impression that Ragnhild had stationed herself there, or been stationed there by others; either way, it was no concern of mine. And when she whispered to me, "Don't say a word, just go quietly down again!" I obeyed, and went to my room.

I had left my window open. I could hear the couple down in the grove, where they sat drinking wine at the stone table; and I could still see the light in Madame's room.

Ten minutes passed; then the light went out.

A moment later I heard hurried footsteps going up the stairs in the house, and involuntarily I looked to see if it was the Captain who had gone up. But the Captain still sat as before.

Next I heard the same footsteps descending the stairs, followed by others. I kept my eye on the front door. The first to emerge was Ragnhild, who came dashing out as if in flight from someone, and headed for the servants' hall. Next came Mrs. Falkenberg with the letter in her hand showing white in the dusk, and her hair down; after her came the engineer. They both sauntered down the drive toward the main road.

Ragnhild burst into my room and flung herself down on a stool, panting with eagerness to tell her story. The strange goings-on she'd been mixed up in that evening, she whispered. Shut the window! Madame and that engineer of hers—no precautions whatsoever—they'd been no more than a hair's breadth away from doing it. He never even let go of Madame when Ragnhild came in with the letter. Ooh! In Madame's own room, with the lamp blown out!

"You're crazy!" I said.

But the sly girl—there was evidently nothing wrong

with her eyes or ears. Spying had become such a habit with her that she couldn't leave off even where Madame was concerned She really was an extraordinary girl.

At first I was virtue incarnate and refused to listen to her slanders What, had she stood there eavesdropping? Shame on her!

What else could she do? she retorted. Her orders were to come in with the letter as soon as her mistress put out the light, and not before. But Madame's windows faced the grove, where the Captain was sitting with Elizabeth from the parsonage. No chance of waiting there. Better to stay on the landing and squint through the keyhole every so often, to see if the light was out.

It no longer sounded so unreasonable.

Suddenly Ragnhild shook her head and said admiringly, "Really, that young dog—nearly getting Madame to…they were only a hair's breadth away!"

What had he nearly got Madame to do? I was pierced by jealousy, I stopped being virtuous, I asked penetrating questions about it all. "What did you say they were doing? How did it all start?"

Ragnhild didn't know how it had started. Madame had told her that a letter was being collected from the cottage, and when it arrived she was to wait until the light in Madame's room went out and then bring it straight up. "Very good," said Ragnhild. "Not until I put out the light, you understand," repeated Madame And Ragnhild had settled down to wait for the letter. But it took ages to come, and she had started thinking, mulling the whole thing over; it was all very strange. Meanwhile, she went up on the landing, hoping to pick up a clue. She could hear Madame and the engineer talking freely together within, and she started listening. Then she squinted through the keyhole and saw Madame was taking down her hair, while the engineer kept saying how lovely she was. Really, that engineer—and then he kissed her!

"On the mouth? Never!"

Ragnhild saw my gross excitement and tried to soothe me.

"On the mouth? Well, perhaps not exactly, but. And the engineer's mouth's nothing to speak of, in my opinion. Why, haven't you shaved beautifully—let's have a look!"

"But what did Madame say to that? Didn't she wriggle free?"

"Yes, I think so. Yes, that's right. And then she screamed."

"Screamed?"

"Yes, right out loud. And the engineer said, 'Sh!'

And every time Madame raised her voice he shut her up again. 'Oh, they're welcome to hear us' was all she'd say; 'there they are themselves, flirting away down in the bushes,' she says—meaning the Captain and Elizabeth from the parsonage. 'Look, there they are!' she says and goes to the window. 'All right, all right,' says the engineer, 'only don't stand there with your hair down.' And he follows her and pulls her back again. Then they start saying all sorts of things, and every time the engineer lowers his voice Madame sings out, 'What did you say?' 'If only you wouldn't scream so loud,' he says, 'it would be nice and quiet here.' Then she shuts up and just smiles at him and sits still. She's quite crazy about him."

"Oh?"

"It stands out a mile. In love with a fellow like that! Then he leans over toward her and puts his hands like this—so!"

"And Madame sat still and let him?"

"Well, more or less. But then she goes to the window again and comes back again; then she goes like this with her tongue and goes right up to him and kisses him. Fancy her wanting to! Because his mouth's nothing to speak of. Then he says, 'Now we're all alone and can hear if anyone's coming.' 'Where's Brother and his lady friend?' she asks. 'Miles and miles away, at the

55

other end of the earth,' he says. And with that he takes hold of her and lifts her up he's that strong, he is. 'Put me down!' she shouts."

"And then what?" I asked breathlessly.

"Why, then you come with the letter, so I don't see any more for the time being. And when I get back to the door, they've turned the key, so it's harder to squint through than ever But I hear Madame say, 'What are you doing? No, we mustn't.' He must have had her in his arms. In the end she says, 'Do wait a bit—put me down for a moment.' So he puts her down. 'Blow out the lamp!' she says. And then it's all dark in the room—ooh!

"But now I was almost at my wits' end what to do," Ragnhild continued. "I stood for a while with my head in a whirl—I thought of knocking on the door straight-away—"

"Of course you should have. What on earth were you waiting for?"

"Don't you see, Madame would have realized I'd been standing at the door," the girl replied. "So I nip off down the stairs. Then I turn around and go back up again, treading heavily so that Madame will hear which way I came from. The door's still fastened; then Madame hears me knocking and comes and opens it.

But the engineer still has hold of her clothes, he's that crazy to get her. 'Don't go, don't go!' he keeps saying, and never once looks my way. Only, when I leave, Madame comes out with me. But merciful heavens, if I hadn't come just when I did! It was touch and go!"

A long, restless night.

When we farmhands came in for our dinner the following day, the maids began whispering about some dust-up there had been between the master and mistress. Ragnhild knew it all. The Captain had noted last night's flowing hair and extinguished lamp; now he laughed and said how nice the hair had looked. Madame kept fairly quiet until she felt sure of herself; then she said, "Well, of course I take my hair down once in a while—it's not yours, is it?" Poor Madame—answering back in a quarrel was not her forte.

Then Elizabeth had come and stuck her nose in, and she was quicker on the draw: rat-tat-tat-tat-tat! Madame managed to say, "All right, we were sitting in the house—but you two were sitting in the bushes!" To which Elizabeth answered sharply, "At least we didn't put out the light!" "What if we did put out the light?" answered Madame. "There's nothing wrong in that—we went out the moment after."

I thought, Good grief, she could have got out of it by saying they put out the light *because* they were going out!

That had been the end of the matter for the time being. But shortly afterward the Captain had hinted at how much older his wife was than Elizabeth. "You should always have your hair down," he said; "I assure you, it made you look positively girlish!" "Yes, I suppose I need to now," answered Madame. But when she saw that Elizabeth was laughing up her sleeve, she became furious and told her to get packing. And Elizabeth put her hands on her hips and said, "My carriage, please, Captain!" To which the Captain replied, "Certainly. And I shall drive you myself."

All this had been overheard by Ragnhild, who was hovering nearby.

I thought to myself, It's clear that they've both been jealous, she over his sitting there in the bushes, he over the flowing hair and extinguished lamp.

As we left the kitchen for a nap, the Captain was busying himself with Elizabeth's carriage. He called to me and said, "I oughtn't to ask you now in your dinner break, but could you go and mend the summerhouse door for me?"

"Very good."

This door had remained unrepaired ever since that

evening when the engineer had burst it open; why did the Captain want it put right just now? He himself could make no use of the summerhouse while he was away with Elizabeth. Was he anxious to deny this retreat to others in his absence? If so, it was a significant move.

I took some tools and materials and went down to the grove.

This was the first time I had inspected the summerhouse from the inside. It was fairly new; it had not been there six years ago. There was plenty of room inside, with pictures on the walls, an alarm clock even (at present run-down), hassocks, tables, a fairsized spring settee upholstered in red plush. The blinds were drawn. First I put a couple of new tiles on the roof, to replace the ones I had broken with the empty bottle. Then I removed the lock to see what the damage was; I had barely started on this when the Captain arrived. Either he had been drinking already or he had a severe hangover.

"There hasn't been any break-in," he said. "Either the door's been left open and has banged violently, or one of the gentlemen who've left stumbled against it in the dark one night. It wouldn't take much to push it open."

But the door had been subjected to considerable

pressure: the lock was broken and the molding on the inside of the door frame damaged.

"Let me have a look," said the Captain. "Put in a new nail here, and compress the spring again." He sat down on a chair.

Mrs. Falkenberg came down the short flight of stone steps into the grove and called, "Is the Captain there?"

"Yes," I said.

She came up, her face trembling with emotion.

"I wanted to talk to you," she said. "Just a quick word or two."

The Captain answered, without getting up, "Go ahead. Do you want to stand or sit?" Then sharply to me, "No, you don't need to go. I haven't got all day."

This must surely mean that he wanted the door mended so that he could take the key with him on his journey.

"I may well have been…I mean, I oughtn't to have said what I did," she began.

The Captain remained silent.

But his remaining silent when she had come here wanting to make it up was more than she could endure, and she ended up saying, "Oh, never mind, it's all the same to me."

And with that she turned to go.

"I thought you wanted to talk to me?" said the Captain.

"Oh, forget it. I really can't be bothered."

"Very well," said the Captain, smiling. He was drunk, no doubt, and irritated about something.

But as she passed me in the doorway she turned to him and said, "You shouldn't go driving off today. There's been enough talk already."

"Well, close your ears to it," he answered.

"That doesn't help in the long run. And it's a disgrace that you don't understand that."

"Well, at least we're both involved in the disgrace," he retorted pertly, glancing around the walls.

I took the lock and went outside.

"You're not going!" the Captain yelled at me. "I've very little time. "

"Oh yes, you've very little time, you're going away again," said Madame. "Only you'd better think it over. I've been thinking things over myself lately; I've given up expecting you to see."

"What do you mean?" he asked. He spoke in arrogant, unaccommodating tones. "What haven't you expected me to see? Your night-time games, when you let down your hair and go blowing out lamps, I suppose? Oh yes, of course."

"I need to go and do some riveting on the anvil," I said, and made a hasty escape.

I stayed away longer than was necessary, but when I returned Madame was still there The voices in the summerhouse had risen, and Madame was saying, "But do you know what I've done? I've lowered myself to showing my jealousy—that's what I've done. Toward the maid, that is—I mean…"

"Yes, go on," said the Captain.

"No no, you don't *want* to understand anything. Have it your own way, then. Only mark my words: you'll have to take the consequences."

Those were her final words. They sounded like an arrow striking against a shield. She went out of the door and walked away.

"Are you managing all right?" the Captain asked me. But I could see that his thoughts were elsewhere and this was merely a facade. A little later he gave an artificial yawn and said, "Dear me, I've got a long drive in front of me. But there it is: Nils won't spare anyone to do it for me."

I had only to replace the lock and put a few nails in the molding and the job was done. The Captain tried the door, put the key in his pocket, thanked me for my work, and went.

Shortly afterward he drove off with Elizabeth.

"Shan't be long!" he called, first to Captain Brother and then to the engineer, waving his hand to them both. "Enjoy yourselves!" he called.

IV

Evening came. What would happen now?

A great deal happened.

We farmhands were sitting at the supper table, while the gentry were having their dinner; and already the dining room was a scene of great merriment and abandon. Ragnhild, who was waiting on them, was in and out with trays of food and bottles; and once when she came out, she giggled, and said to the other maids, "I do believe even Madame is drunk tonight."

I had neither slept the previous night nor had my afternoon rest that day; in addition, the latest events had affected me and preyed on my peace of mind. So when I had finished my supper I wandered off into the forest, in order to sit for a while on my own. And there I stayed for a long time.

I looked down toward the manor. Now the Captain was away, the servants in bed, the beasts in the stables and barns sleeping soundly. Fat Captain Brother and his lady had doubtless found themselves a hideout the moment dinner was over; old and fat he may have been, and the lady no longer young, but he was after her like a firebrand. That left only Mrs. Falkenberg and the young engineer; and where might they be now?

Their pigeon.

I drifted back home, yawning and shivering in the cool night air, and went up to my room. Soon afterward Ragnhild came and asked me to stay awake and lend a helping hand if the need arose. It was all so unpleasant tonight, she explained; the people in the house were doing just as they pleased, walking around in their underwear from room to room, drunk. Was Madame drunk too? Yes, she was. Was she, too, walking around in her underwear? No, but Captain Brother was, and Madame was saying "Bravo!" And the engineer was. They were quite mad, all four of them. And now, drunk as they were, Ragnhild had just gone and taken them two more bottles of wine.

"Come with me and hear for yourself!" said Ragnhild. "Now they've gone up to Madame's room."

"No, I'm going to bed," I answered. "And so should you."

"But if they ring for something all of a sudden?"

"Let them ring!"

Then Ragnhild revealed that the Captain himself had asked her to stay up that night, in case Madame should need her.

This changed the whole situation at a stroke. The Captain must have had his fears and left Ragnhild to keep watch. I put on my smock again and accompanied her across to the manor.

We stopped on the upstairs landing; we could hear sounds of great merriment coming from Madame's room. But Madame herself spoke clearly and distinctly, and was certainly not drunk. "Yes, she is," Ragnhild insisted; "she's acting ever so strange."

I would dearly have liked to see Madame for a moment.

Ragnhild and I went down to the kitchen and sat there. But my mind was ill at ease, and soon I took the lamp from the wall and told Ragnhild to follow me. We went upstairs again.

"Now ask Madame to come out here and see me," I said.

"Why, whatever for?"

"I've got a message for her."

And Ragnhild knocked and went in.

Only then did I start thinking what sort of message I might give. I could simply look Madame in the eye and say, "The Captain asked me to send you his greetings." Would that do? Or I could say, "The Captain had no choice but to drive himself, because Nils wouldn't spare anyone else."

But a moment can sometimes last an age and the brain work with the speed of lightning. I had time to reject both these plans and conceive a third before Madame came out—though I doubt if my last plan was any better than the first two.

Madame asked in tones of astonishment, "Well, what is it?"

And Ragnhild came with her and looked questioningly at me.

I held the lamp out toward Madame and said, "Excuse my coming so late, but I'm going to the post office first thing tomorrow, and thought perhaps Madame might have some letters for me to post."

"Letters? No," she replied, shaking her head.

She seemed preoccupied, but not in the least drunk. But perhaps she was merely keeping her end up.

"No, I've no letters," she repeated, and made as if to return to her room.

"Then I beg your pardon," I said.

"Is it for the Captain you're going?"

"No, for myself."

She moved away. While still in the doorway she said to her guests in an offended tone, "That was a pure fabrication!"

Ragnhild and I went down again. I had seen Madame.

But my present humiliation! Nor was I greatly soothed by something which Ragnhild now let slip—which, indeed, fairly made me shrivel up. It appeared that the good Ragnhild's story about the Captain setting her to keep watch had been sheer hocus-pocus. She maintained that I had misunderstood her, but my suspicion grew stronger and clearer: that Ragnhild was spying, tonight as at other times, entirely on her own account, purely for the love of it.

I retired to my room. Look what my unseemly officiousness had done! Pure fabrication, Madame had called it—she must have seen through me. I promised myself ruefully that from now on I would leave everything and everyone to their own devices.

I threw myself fully dressed on my bed.

After a while I heard through the open window Mrs. Falkenberg out in the courtyard, talking loudly. The engineer was with her, answering from time to time. Madame was in raptures over the fine weather, the warm evening, and how lovely it was out here—so infinitely nicer than indoors!

But now her voice seemed to be getting less clear.

I ran to the window and saw them both standing by the stone steps down to the grove. There seemed to be something the engineer had not yet managed to get off his chest. "Please listen to me for a moment," he said.

There followed a short and urgent appeal, which was duly answered; indeed rewarded. She had been deaf to him so long that now he spoke as if to someone hard of hearing. They stood there by the steps, and neither gave a thought to anyone else in the whole world. Listen who dared, watch who dared—the night belonged to them, their words belonged to them, the very spring seemed to force them together. He was like a cat, all poised to throw himself upon her; every movement she made fired him afresh. And as the moment for action came nearer, there was a crude force in his desire for her. The young firebrand!

"I've pleaded with you long enough," he said breathlessly. "Yesterday you nearly said yes; today you're deaf again. Your idea is that you and Brother and Auntie and all the rest should enjoy yourselves, quite innocently of course, while I sit and watch—the ladies' tame cavalier. But by God in heaven, no! You lie before my eyes like a pleasure garden, only there's a miserable fence around the garden, with a gate—shall I tell you what I'm going to do with that gate?"

"No, what?" she asked. "No, you've drunk too much, Hugo—you're so young. We've both drunk too much."

"And then you start playing an underhanded game with me, sending a special messenger for a letter that simply can't wait—yet you can have the heart to raise my hopes, to promise me—"

"I shall never do it again."

"Never do it again? What does that mean? I've seen you go up to a man—myself, as it happens—seen you come up to me—your tongue had a life of its own Christ, how you kissed me! So just keep quiet about never doing it again, it's done now, I can still feel it, the most fantastic sensation—thank you for giving it to me…You're still going around with that letter next to your breast—let me see it!"

"You're so violent, Hugo. No, it's getting late, we must break it up."

"Will you let me see that letter?"

"Why should I? Certainly not!"

He made as if to use force, but checked himself and spat out, "What? You won't? You're an absolute—I won't say bitch, but maybe something worse—"

" Hugo!"

" Precisely."

"If you *must* see the letter, here it is!" She thrust her hand inside her blouse, drew out the letter, un-folded it, waved it at him; he should see how innocent she was. "Here's the letter. It's from my mother—look, there's the signature. It's from Mama. Well?"

It was as if she had boxed his ears. All he could say

was, "From Mama? But then it can't have been so important, surely?"

"There, you can see for yourself! Well, perhaps not *that* important, still…"

He leaned against the paling and began grappling with the problem.

"I see, from your mother. It was a letter from your mother that came and interrupted us. Do you know what I think? You've cheated me. You've fooled me from beginning to end. The light's beginning to dawn."

She tried to find a way out. "It really was an important letter; Mama's coming here on a visit, quite soon now. And I was waiting to hear."

"You cheated me, didn't you?" he resumed. "You arranged for the letter to come just at the right moment, when we'd put out the lamp. That's it. You just wanted to get me excited. You had your maid there, guarding you."

"Oh, do be reasonable! Let's go in now—it's getting so late."

"Who's being unreasonable? Well, maybe I did have a drop too much up there, and now I'm not expressing myself clearly."

He could think only of the letter, and now he came back to it again. "And besides, there was no need to make such a deadly secret of a letter from your Mama.

No, I see it all now. You want to go, do you? Very well then, go, madam. Good night, madam. My filial regards."

He bowed and remained standing there, sneering.

"Filial? Yes, because I'm old," she answered; and now she was deeply agitated. "And you're so young, Hugo; yes, it's true. And that's why I kissed you. I couldn't be your mother, of course; still, I'm much, much older than you. But I'm not all *that* old; you'd see that if…But I'm older than Elizabeth and the rest. What am I saying? It's not true at all. I don't know what else the years may have done to me, but they haven't made me old. Well? Do you think they have? What do you know about these things in any case?"

"No no," he said evasively. "But is there any sense in going on like this? Here you are, day after day, you're young, you've nothing else to do except keep guard over yourself and get others to do the same. And God knows, you promised me something—but that means little to you; it tickles your vanity keeping me dangling and lashing me with your great white wings."

"Great white wings," she murmured to herself.

"Yes. Or perhaps they're great red wings. Look at you standing there now—beautiful, all right, but fit for nothing."

"Oh dear, I know I've drunk far too much. But

71

there's plenty of things I'm fit for." Suddenly she took his hand and drew him down the steps. I heard her say, "Why should I care? Does he imagine Elizabeth's so much better?"

They came up the path as far as the summerhouse. Here she hesitated and stopped.

"No, where are we going?" she asked. "Ha-ha, we must be mad! You wouldn't have thought I was mad, would you? I'm not, either—well, yes, now and again. There, the door's locked; come, let's go. What a mean trick to lock the door when we want to go in!"

Full of bitterness and suspicion, he answered, "You're cheating again. You knew very well the door was locked."

"You really must stop thinking so rottenly of me all the time, do you hear? But why should he lock the summerhouse so carefully and have it all to himself? Yes, I *did* know the door was locked, that's why I came here with you. I daren't. No, Hugo, I won't, you must believe me. Are you crazy? Come away!"

She took his hand again and tried to turn back. They struggled for a bit; he didn't want to follow. Then he threw both arms overpoweringly around her, and kissed her again and again. She yielded more and more ground, punctuating the kisses with broken words.

"I've never kissed another man before, never—I

swear to God—you must believe me—I've never kissed—"

"No, of course not," he answered impatiently, taking her with him step by step.

At the summerhouse he released her for a moment, gave the door a hard heave with his shoulder, and broke it open for the second time. Then, with a single stride, he was beside her again. Neither of them spoke.

Even in the doorway she still resisted, clinging to the frame and not letting go.

"No, I've never been unfaithful to him, I won't, I've never, never—"

He pulled her toward him, kissed her for a full minute, two minutes, passionately and without pause; she bent backward under his weight, her hand slipped on the doorframe, she let go…

A white mist drifted in front of my eyes. So—now they were there. Now he was unfolding her. Now he was taking his will and pleasure with her…

A mournful lassitude descended on me; I was alone with my pain. It was late; my heart had gone to rest.

Through the white mist I saw a leaping figure: it was Ragnhild emerging from the bushes. As she ran, her tongue was hanging out.

The engineer came up to me, nodded a good morning, and asked if I would mend the summerhouse door.

"Is it broken again?"

"Yes, it got broken last night."

It was early in the morning—not more than half-past four—and we farmhands had not yet set out for the fields. The engineer's eyes looked small, and glittered as if they were smarting; they had doubtless seen no sleep. He offered no explanation of the door's being broken.

For Captain Falkenberg's sake rather than for his, I went straight down to the summerhouse to put the door in order for the second time. There was probably no hurry—the Captain had a long way to drive, there and back; still, it would soon be twenty-four hours since he had left home.

The engineer came with me. Without at the time quite knowing why, I received a favorable impression of him: all right, he had broken the door in last night, but he was not the man to sneak out of the affair afterward—he and nobody else had got it mended. Perhaps he had merely flattered my vanity by the confidence he showed in my silence. That was it. That was why I formed a good impression.

"I'm an Inspector of Log Driving on the watercourses," said the engineer. "How long are you staying here?"

"Not long. Till the end of the season."

"If you want, you can get a job with me."

This was an occupation with which I was quite unfamiliar. Besides, it was not log drivers and proletariat that I cared to be with but men who tilled the soil or tended the forests. However, I thanked the engineer for his offer.

"It's very good of you to fix the door. The fact is, I wanted a gun and was looking everywhere for one—I wanted to do some shooting. Then I thought, Maybe the Captain keeps a gun in here."

I made no answer. I would have preferred him to say nothing.

"So I wanted to ask you before you went out in the fields," he concluded.

I mended and replaced the lock once again, and started hammering in more nails where the molding had again been splintered. While I was busy with this we heard Captain Falkenberg in the courtyard and caught a glimpse of him through the bushes, unhitching and stabling the horses.

The engineer started, fumbled for his watch, and took it out, while his eyes became large and vacant, as if they saw nothing. Suddenly he said, "No, I really must…I was forgetting…"

Then he disappeared far away down the garden.

So he was sneaking out of it after all!

The next moment the Captain came up. He was pale, covered in dust, bleary-eyed from lack of sleep, but completely sober. While still some way off he asked, "How did you get in there?"

I raised my cap and said nothing.

"Has the door been broken in again?"

"It was just—I suddenly remembered I'd been short of a couple of nails yesterday. It's done now. If the Captain would care to lock up now."

Fool that I was! If I couldn't think of a better excuse than that, he was bound to put two and two together.

He stood for a few seconds looking at the door with narrowed eyes. He must have had his suspicions; but then he put the key in the keyhole, locked the door, and went. There was nothing else he could do.


V


All the guests had departed: fat Captain Brother, the lady with the shawl, Engineer Lassen. And Captain Falkenberg was at last ready to join his regiment. I thought: He must have applied for a deferment and had a very good case, or he would have left long ago.

During the last few days we farmhands had got through an immense amount of work; it had been a strain on both man and beast. But Nils had wanted it that way, and knew what he was doing: he wished to gain time for another purpose.

One day he set me to work raking and cleaning and tidying all the way around the various buildings. This used up just about all the time gained, if not more; but somehow it improved the whole appearance of the place. And this was Nils's aim: to cheer the Captain up a little before he left home. After a while I began, on my own initiative, fastening the odd crosspiece in the garden fence that had worked loose, or straightening up an outbuilding door that had warped. Finally I started preparing two new beams for the ramp to the hayloft.

"Where are you going when you leave here?" the Captain asked me.

"I don't know. I shall wander around."

"I could do with you here for a while; there's a lot to be done."

"Is the Captain thinking of painting by any chance?"

"That too. No, I'm not sure about that. It will cost a lot of money to paint all these buildings. No, there was something else I had in mind. Do you know anything about timber? Can you select and mark trees for felling?"

So he was still pretending he hadn't recognized me from the last time I worked in his woods. But had he still got any trees left to fell?

"Oh yes, I'm used to timber. Where does the Captain mean to fell this year?"

"Everywhere. Anywhere. There must be something left."

"Very good."

Next I put the new beams in the hayloft ramp, and when I had finished that, I took down the flagpole and fixed it with a knob and a halyard. Øvrebø was already looking more shipshape, and Nils announced that he was beginning to feel like a new man. I got him to go to the Captain and put in a good word for the painting, but the Captain looked at him anxiously and said, "Yes, yes. But there's other things besides painting and painting, you know. Let's wait until the autumn and see what the harvest's like, after all the sowing we've done this year."

But when the flagpole stood there with the old paint scraped off and a new knob and halyard, even the Captain noticed, and telegraphed to order paint. Not that there was any hurry; an ordinary letter would have done.

Two days passed. The paint arrived but was put to one side: we still had a lot of seasonal work to do.

During this period we even used the Captain's two

carriage horses on the harrow and the seeder; and when it came to planting potatoes, Nils had to enlist the help of all the maids. The Captain agreed to this and to everything else; then he went off to join his regiment. After that we were on our own.

But before he left there was a great matrimonial scene.

We all knew of the disharmony between the pair of them; and Ragnhild and the dairymaid went around talking openly about it. The crops were coming on nicely now, the pastures grew daily more lush, the spring was fine and favorable to growth; but Øvrebø was also a scene of strife. There were times when Madame went around with a tear-stained face, or with an exaggeratedly haughty air, as if to say she had given up crawling to anyone. Her mother came, a mild lady with spectacles on her white mouse face; but she didn't stay long—only a few days—before returning to her home in Kristiansand. She made out that the air here didn't suit her.

That matrimonial scene: it had been a final, bitter, hour-long altercation. Ragnhild gave us the full story afterward; there were no raised voices, but both the Captain and Madame had spoken in strong, measured terms; and in their bitterness they had agreed to go their separate ways.

"You don't mean it!" said the assembled company in the kitchen, clasping their hands.

Ragnhild put on an air and started impersonating the protagonists.

"'You were involved in breaking the summerhouse door again?' says the Captain. 'Yes,' says Madame. 'And what else?' he asks. 'Everything!' says Madame. So the Captain smiles and says, 'Well, that's a plain, straight-forward answer—it doesn't take long to work out what that means.' Madame says nothing. 'What merit does that young whelp possess—beyond the fact that he once helped me out of a jam?' asks the Captain. Madame gives him a look and says, 'He helped you?' 'Yes,' says the Captain, 'he countersigned a loan for me.' And Madame says, 'I never knew that.' But then the Captain says, 'Has he really never told you?' Madame shakes her head. 'But what of that?' he goes on; 'would it have made any difference if you'd known?' First she says yes, then she says no. 'Are you in love with him?' he asks. 'Are you in love with Elizabeth?' she answers back. 'Yes,' says the Captain; then he sits there, smiling. 'Good!' says Madame, sullen-like. Then they say noth-ing for quite a while, till the Captain starts up again and says, 'You were right when you said I ought to think things over; now I've done so. I'm not addicted to drink; it's a funny thing, but I've never really enjoyed living it up. All the same, I've done just that. But now I'm through with it!' 'How nice for you!' says Madame, sullenlike again. 'Yes,' he says, 'but it would have been nicer still if you'd shown yourself just a tiny bit pleased.' 'You'd better get Elizabeth to show herself pleased,' she says. He just says 'Elizabeth!' and keeps shaking his head. After that they sit quiet again for a while. Then the Captain asks her, 'What are you going to do now?' 'Look, don't you worry about me,' says Madame, very slow and deliberate-like; 'I can become a nurse if you want, or I can cut my hair short and become a schoolteacher if you want.' 'If I want!' he says—'No, you must make up your own mind.' 'I need to know first what you propose to do,' she says. 'I propose to stay where I am,' he says; 'you're the one who's thrown yourself out,' he says. And Madame nods and says, 'Very well.'"

The entire kitchen gasped. "Ye gods!" said Nils; "but surely it'll all come right again." He looked around to see what the rest of us thought.

For the first two days after the Captain's departure, Madame sat playing her piano all day long. On the third, Nils drove her to the station; she was going to her mother in Kristiansand. After that we were still more on our own. Madame had taken none of her things with her. Perhaps she felt she owned nothing;

or perhaps everything had come from the Captain in the first place and she wished to have none of it. Oh, how sad it all was!

Ragnhild had been told by Madame that she needn't leave. However, it was the cook who took charge of everything and kept the keys. It was best for us all that way.

On Saturday the Captain came home on leave—something which, according to Nils, he had never done before. Despite his wife's absence he held himself erect; and he was as sober as a judge. He gave me clear, concise instructions about the trees I should mark, coming out with me and pointing here and there: battens and batten ends, a thousand dozen. He would be away three weeks this time, he told me. On Sunday afternoon he went off again. By now he was more decisive in manner, more like himself.

At last the plowing and sowing were over, and the potatoes in the ground. Now Nils and the boy could manage the day-to-day work on their own and I was able to start marking trees.

I was as happy as the days were long. We had a warm, rainy spell that made the woods all wet; I never let this keep me indoors but went out just the same. Then the hot weather set in, and during the long evenings after I got home I would take pleasure in going around and putting things to rights: here a gutter, there a window that was hanging crooked. Finally I raised the fire ladder and started to scrape the old peeling paint off the north wall of the barn. It would be a joke if, after all, I managed to paint the barn before the summer was out. The paint was there!

But now a new factor caused me to weary of the work and of the whole place. It was not the same working here now as it had been when the master and mistress were at home; I knew from experience, and was reminded again, that it is good to have someone over you in a job—unless, that is, you yourself have been placed in charge. The maids had no one now to be in awe of; Ragnhild and the dairymaid were boisterous at table, and had quarrels which the cook did not always possess the authority to quell. All this made for an unpleasant atmosphere. In addition, somebody must have gone and spoken about me to my former good comrade Lars Falkenberg, and sown suspicion of me in his heart.

Lars came to the manor one evening, took me aside, and forbade me to come to his cottage in future. His manner was comical and threatening.

I had been to his home occasionally with washing—perhaps half a dozen times in all; he himself had been out, but Emma and I had chatted about old topics and new. The last time I was there Lars had suddenly come home and at once taken Emma to task for sitting there on a stool in her petticoat. "It's too hot for a skirt," she replied. "Yes, and your hair's wandered halfway down your back," he said; "I suppose that's because of the heat, too?" He really had it in for her. Nor did he answer my "good night" when I left.

Since then I had not been there. So what had made him come here this evening? Ragnhild must have been busy again with her spy's tongue.

After forbidding me in so many words to darken his door again, Lars nodded and looked at me as if I ought to drop dead.

"What's more, I understand Emma's been down here," he went on. "She won't do that again, I rather think."

"She may have been here once or twice with washing."

"That's right, blame it on the washing. And then you come to the cottage yourself several times a week with washing—a shirt one time, a pair of underpants the next. But from now on Ragnhild can do your washing for you."

"All right, all right."

"No sirree! I know you—coming to people's homes and getting too friendly when you find they're alone! No, thank you very much!"

Nils came up; he must have realized what was going on and, like the good friend he was, wanted to help me. He heard the last few words and at once declared in my favor that he had never once seen me do anything I shouldn't, all the time I had been there.

But Lars Falkenberg at once drew himself up to his full height and measured Nils with a disdainful eye. He had, indeed, a long-standing grudge against the foreman: Able though Lars had shown himself since acquiring his own little property up in the forest, Nils had done far better work down here on the Captain's estate. And this rankled with Lars Falkenberg.

"What are you sticking your ugly mug in here for?" he asked.

"I'm only saying what happens to be true," answered Nils.

"You are, are you, jackass? You make me want to puke all over you."

At this Nils and I took ourselves off, while Lars continued to belabor us with words. Needless to say, Ragnhild stood sniffing the lilacs as we passed.

That evening I began to think I would resume my wanderings as soon as I had finished my work in the forest. The Captain came after three weeks, as he had said, and praised me for scraping the paint off the north wall of the barn. "I can see it's going to end with your repainting it too," he said. I told him how much timber I had marked, and reported that there was not much left to do. "Carry on marking!" was his answer. Then he rejoined his regiment for another three weeks.

But I had no desire to spend another three weeks at Øvrebø now. I marked enough trees to make a few score dozen more, and reckoned it all up on my work sheet: it would have to do. But it was still too early to live in the woods and hills: there were flowers but no berries; mating birds with their chirrup and song, butterflies, flies and midges, but no cloudberries, no angelica.

Here I was, in a town.*

I had called on Engineer Lassen, Inspector of Log Driving, and he had kept his promise and given me work, even though the season was far advanced. To begin with, I had to do a tour of the river, marking on a map the points where the worst logjams had occurred. The engineer was a straightforward enough fellow; merely very young still. He plied me with superfluous good advice on matters about which he thought I was ignorant; this made him feel more grown-up.

So this man had helped Captain Falkenberg out of

---

*   From the description, the town would appear to be Drammen, at the head of Drammenfiord, southwest of Oslo.—Trans.

a jam! Now, probably, the Captain regretted this and wanted to free himself; hence the felling of his timber down to the last batten. And I, too, wished him free; I even began reproaching myself for not having marked down another few days' timber, for stinting the help I had given. Supposing, now, it proved just a fraction too little!

Engineer Lassen was clearly a man of means, living as he did in a hotel, where he had two rooms. I only saw his office, but even this was expensively appointed—books and magazines, a silver writing set, a gilt theodolite, and so on; his silk-lined summer topcoat hung on the wall. Beyond doubt, he was one of the town's richer and more important citizens; there was even a large picture of him in the local photographer's display case.

Of an afternoon, moreover, I would see him taking the air with the young ladies of the town. As supreme head of logdriving operations, he liked best of all to stroll out onto the 475-foot bridge over the rapids, where he would stop to peer upstream and downstream. Just here—around the piers of the bridge and on the flat rocks downstream—was where the logs were most inclined to jam, and for this reason alone the engineer kept a team of log drivers almost constantly on call. When he stood on the bridge surveying the men out on the logjam, he was like a ship's captain, young, strong, and able to command. His fair companions would wait patiently on the bridge, however strong the current below. And to hear each other speak above the roar of the torrent they had often to lean their heads together.

But it was precisely when the engineer took up his station on the bridge, and stood there turning fore and aft, that he lost he stature and elegance: his athlete's build and tight-fitting jacket that pinched at the back conspired to make his bottom quite absurdly large.

The very first evening, when he had already briefed me for my journey upriver in the morning, I met him promenading with two ladies. At the sight of me he stopped, halted his retinue, and gave me the same instructions all over again. "Lucky I met you," he said. "Because tomorrow you must be up early. Take a pike pole with you and free as much timber as you can. If any logjam is more than you can manage, mark it on the map—got the map, have you? And carry on until you meet my other man working his way down. But remember to mark in red, not blue. And make sure you do the work properly." Then to the ladies: "This is a man I've appointed to work under me; I really can't be bothered traipsing everywhere myself."

How busily engaged he was! He even took out a

notebook and made a note. He was so young, and had such a charming retinue to show off to.

Next morning I started out early; by the time it was light, at four o'clock, I was already a fair distance up the river. I had food with me, and my pike pole—which is the same as a boat hook.

Here was no young, luxuriant growth as at Øvrebø; the forest floor was barren and stony, heather and pine needles covered the ground for mile after mile. The felling had been ruthless, the pulp mills too greedy in their demands, a load of scantling was all that remained; and the virtual absence of young trees made this a dreary landscape that I wandered through.

By midday I had cleared several small jams and marked in one large one. I ate some food, drank from the river, and after a short rest continued on my way. Toward evening I came to a biggish logjam where a man was at work. This was the man I was scheduled to meet. I didn't at once come forward but amused myself for a while watching him furtively. He guarded his life with the utmost care, and was even afraid of getting his feet wet. The first hint of danger, of being carried out into the stream on a loosened log—and he was away. Then I went right up close and looked at him—and yes, it was my good friend Grindhusen.

Grindhusen, my companion at Skreia in the days

of my youth; Grindhusen, my well-digging partner of six years ago.

And now here he was again.

We exchanged greetings, we sat on the logjam and talked, we questioned and answered for the space of an hour. By then it was too late to do more work that day, so we got up and walked a short distance up along the river to where Grindhusen had his little wooden hut. We crept in, lit a fire, made coffee, and had a meal. Then we went out again, lit our pipes, and lay full length in the heather.

Grindhusen had become old; he was in just the same plight as I, and he didn't at all care to remember the gay nights we had danced through in our youth. He it was who had been after the girls like a red-haired wolf; now he was well chastened by age and toil, and he had even ceased to smile. If I had had some brandy with me, he might have livened up, but I had none.

In his younger days Grindhusen had been as stubborn and awkward as they come; now he was mild and stupid. "Maybe, maybe" was his answer to everything; "you're right, you know, dead right," he would say— not because he meant it but because life had made him evasive and vacillating. It was unpleasant meeting him again; evasive and vacillating—that is what life makes us all, year by year.

One day followed another, he said, but where he was concerned things weren't what they used to be; he'd suffered lately from rheumatism, also from heartburn—cardialgia, they called it. Still, as long as he could keep this job with Engineer Lassen, he'd just about manage; he knew the river all the way up, and spent the whole spring and early summer here in his hut. As for clothes, he wore nothing but trousers and smocks, summer and winter. Oh, and last year he'd been lucky, he suddenly told me: he'd found a sheep that didn't belong to anyone. Sheep in the forest? "Up there!" he answered, pointing. He'd had mutton on Sundays from that sheep till far into the winter. Mind you, he had people in America now, that wasn't the problem, children who'd married and settled nicely. They'd sent him a little help the first year or so—but then they'd stopped, and now it was close on two years since they'd even written. Yes, that was the way it was for him and his wife in their old age.

Grindhusen grew pensive.

There came a faint soughing from the forest and from the river, as of millions of nothings flowing ceaselessly away. No birds dwelt here, no animals frisked around; but when I rolled a stone aside I would find some crawling insect underneath. "Can you understand what these tiny creatures live on?" I asked. "What tiny creatures?" said Grindhusen; "they're only ants and the like." "It's some kind of beetle," I said; "put him on the grass and roll a stone over him and he'll live." Grindhusen answered, "Maybe, maybe." But he hadn't paid my words the slightest heed. So I pursued the line of thought for myself: slip an ant under the same stone, however, and soon there will be no more beetle.

And the forest and the river went on soughing—one eternity agreeing with another eternity about something. In tempest and thunder, however, there is war between them.

"Yes, that's the way it is," said Grindhusen at long last; "it'll be two years come the fourteenth of August since I got the last letter. There was a nice photograph inside, from Olea—she lives in Dakota, as they call it. A swell photograph, that was, but could I sell it? Ah well, with God's help something will turn up," said Grindhusen with a yawn. "What was I going to say—how much are you getting per day?"

"I don't know."

But Grindhusen gave me a suspicious look, thinking I was reluctant to tell him.

"Well, it's all the same to me," he said. "I was only asking."

So I guessed a figure, just to satisfy him. "I suppose I'll get a couple of kroner, two or three kroner?"

"Yes, I dare say you will," he said enviously. "I only get two kroner, mind, and I'm an old hand at this game."

But now he must have become nervous lest I noise his discontent abroad, for he started boasting about Engineer Lassen, how he was a damned fine fellow in every respect—"He'd never do me an injustice. A likely idea, indeed! Why, he's been like a father to me, that I will say for him."

The engineer a father to Grindhusen! It sounded ineffably droll, coming from that almost toothless mouth. I could doubtless have learned a thing or two about the engineer from this source, but I asked no questions.

"He didn't say anything about me coming down into town?" asked Grindhusen.

"No."

"There's times he sends for me, all in aid of nothing in particular—just wants to chat with me a bit. A mighty good sort, he is."

Dusk gathered. Grindhusen yawned again, crept into the hut, and bedded down.

Next morning we cleared the logjam. "Come with me up my way for a bit," said Grindhusen. So off we went. After walking for an hour we saw buildings and fields: a hill farm up in the woods. Some association of ideas made me think of Grindhusen's sheep.

"Was it somewhere about here you found that sheep?" I asked.

Grindhusen gave me a look.

"Here? Lord no. That was miles from here—over Trovatn way. "

"Isn't Trovatn in the next parish?"

"That's right. So it's miles and miles from here."

But now Grindhusen wished me to come no farther with him; he stopped and thanked me for my company. Surely I could come as far as the farm, I objected; but Grindhusen wasn't even calling at the farm—a place he never set foot in. I was left alone with the day, and the long walk into town.

So I turned and went back the way I had come.


# VI


This was not my idea of work at all: walking and walking along the riverbank, upstream and downstream, clearing the smaller jams, then on again. And at the end of each trip, fetching up back at my boardinghouse in town. During this period I had only one man to talk to: the underporter at the engineer's hotel, a giant of a man with childlike eyes, and hands that could span eleven inches. He had fallen and hit his head when he was small, he told me, and had never got further in life than heaving and carrying heavy loads. With him I exchanged a few words from time to time, and with no one else.

That little town!

When the river was high, it raged and roared through the middle of the town, dividing it in two. North and south of the roar, people lived in their wooden houses, apparently scraping a livelihood from day to day. Of the many children who crossed the bridge or ran errands to the shops, none went naked, few probably suffered any want, all were good-looking. Most amusing of all were the older girls, tall and thin and bony, cheerfully absorbed in each other and their own little world. Sometimes they would stop on the bridge to watch the men down on the logjam, and help them as they hauled at the timber by singing "Yo-o heave ho!" Then they would giggle and dig each other in the ribs.

But no birds sang.

Strange, this absence of birds. On quiet evenings, at sundown, the great enclosed log pond lay there, deep, its surface immobile; midges and butterflies swarmed over it; the trees on the bank were mirrored in it; but no birds perched in the trees. Perhaps the deafening roar of the torrent was to blame: no birds could thrive where they could not hear each other sing. And that was why the only winged creatures here were midges and flies—though God alone knows why even the crows and the magpies shunned our town.

Every small town has its daily event that people turn out for; so, for that matter, does every big town that boasts a promenade. On the west coast it is the mail boat; how hard it is to live there and keep away from the quay when the boat comes in! Here, in this inland town a full twenty miles from the sea, and only hills and mountains all around, we had the river. Had the water risen or fallen during the night? Would they be clearing logs from the booms today? How absorbing we found it! To be sure, we also had a narrow-gauge railroad, but this was nothing to write home about: the line ended here, it went as far as it could, then stopped, like a cork in a bottle. And the tiny little cars were enchanting, but people were bashful about objects so ridiculously old and stunted—why, one could hardly sit upright in them with a hat on.

And then of course there were the markets and churches and schools and post offices; and sawmills and pulp mills all along the river. As for grocery stores, their number was beyond belief.

We had this, we had that. I was a stranger here—as everywhere—yet I could count a multitude of things we had in addition to the river. Had the town once been a big one? No, it has remained small for two hundred and fifty years. Once, however, there was a greater man over all the lesser men—a grander who rode with a servant behind and forded it over many an acre. Now we were all equal—except, perhaps, for Engineer Lassen, this twenty-something-year-old Inspector of Log Driving who could afford two rooms at his hotel.

Having nothing to do, I caught myself meditating as follows: Here stands a great house, about two hundred years old, once the home of the wealthy Ole Olsen Ture; a huge two-story house the length of a block, now used as a depot. At the time when this house was built, there was plenty of massive timber in these parts; three beams together made the height of a man; they were filled with ore, with iron, and would blunt any ax. And inside there were halls and cells, as in a castle. Here the great Ture reigned like a monarch.

Times changed. It was no longer enough for a house to be big and to afford shelter from cold and rain; it had also to give pleasure to the eye. On the opposite side of the river stands an old archaic building with a nicely balanced Empire-style veranda, complete with pillars and a pediment. It is not beyond criticism, but it is beautiful in its way, and stands out like a white temple against the green hills behind. And there is yet another house which I have stopped to look at, near the marketplace. Its double door onto the street has ancient handles and cut-glass rococo mirrors; but the frame around these mirrors is fluted in the style of Louis XVI. The cartouche over the door bears the date 1795 in arabic figures—the transitional period has arrived! Even in this little town there were people in those days who kept abreast of the times, without the aid of the telegraph or of steam.

But later generations built against snow and rain, and for no other purpose. The houses were neither large nor beautiful. They were intended, Swiss-fashion, to provide a dwelling place for wife and children; and that was all. From this wretched little people up in the Alps, which throughout its history has never been anything or done anything, we learned to set no store by how a human dwelling looked to the eye, as long as it went down well with globe-trotting tourists. Why get excited because the white building on the hillside has something of a temple's peace and beauty? Why preserve the great big house from Ole Olsen Ture's days, when it could make way for twenty little homes?

Things have gone downhill until they have reached rock bottom. Now cobblers are filled with glee, not because we have all grown equally great, but because we have all grown equally small. Our pigeon!

The long bridge is excellent for walking on, being paved with planks and as even as a floor; any young lady can walk gracefully here. It is airy, too, and open at the sides—the perfect vantage point for inquisitive people like me.

Shouts rise to us from the men down there on the logjam, as they struggle to free the timber that has caught on rocks and boulders in the river. Log after log comes drifting down, to join the logs already stuck there; the jam grows and grows, until there may be a couple of hundred dozen balks at a single spot on the river. If all goes well, the men can free them again in a reasonably short time; if things go badly, some unfortunate driver may even be carried down the rapids to his death.

Out on the logjam are ten men with boat hooks, all of them more or less wet from falling in. The foreman points to the log which needs freeing next; but at times we spectators recognize signs of dissent among the gang of drivers. The din prevents our hearing anything; but there are clearly those who favor freeing some quite different log first, and one old hand has started voicing his discontent. Knowing his language, I seem to hear him say, stubbornly and deliberately, "Happen we'd do better to take him first!" Now ten pairs of eyes are cast on the new log, working out a fairway for it through the magpie's nest of other logs; if all agree, ten boat hooks descend on it. For a moment these boat hooks extend from the log like the strings of a harp. Then there is a cry of "Heave!" they all pull, and the log moves forward a little. Fresh grips, another cry, and again it moves forward a little. It is like watching ten ants at work on a twig. Finally the log sails down over the rapids.

But certain logs are almost immovable, and often it is just such a log, and no other, which has to be freed first of all. Then the drivers fan out and surround it, digging their boat hooks in wherever it is visible in its magpie's nest, some pulling, others pushing; if it is dry they splash water over it by way of lubrication. And the boat hooks no longer extend from the log in regular formation, like strings on a harp, but radiate from it crisscross in all directions, like a spider's web.

At times the ten-man chorus on the river can be heard all day long, except during meals; at times, indeed, we hear them for days on end. Then suddenly a new sound falls on the ear: the stroke of an ax. Some swine of a log has settled so awkwardly that it cannot be dragged clear. And yet it is holding the entire mass together; therefore, it has to be cut. Not many blows are needed; the immense pressure brought to bear soon causes it to crack, and the huge magpie's nest caves in and starts turning around. At once the men break off and stand at the ready; if the section they are on breaks loose, they must move with catlike agility to a safer place. Every day, every hour of their work is fraught with fearful tension; their lives depend entirely on themselves.

But this is a dead-alive little town.

It is a sad spectacle, a dead town trying to pretend it is alive. It is the same with Bruges, that great city of former years; likewise with many cities in Holland, southern Germany, northern France, the Orient. Standing in the marketplace of such a town, you say to yourself, This town was alive once—and look, I can still see people walking about in its streets!

It is very strange: our town is tucked away, shut in by mountains; yet it seems to possess its share of female beauty and male ambition, just like any other town. Only it's a queer, mysterious life, the life lived here, with short crooked fingers, mouse eyes, and ears filled day and night with the everlasting roar from the torrent. A beetle walks in the heather, occasional blades of yellowing grass loom up—great trees they seem to the beetle! Two local merchants are walking across the bridge, doubtless on their way to the post office. To-day they have clubbed together to buy a whole sheet of postage stamps at one go, for the sake of the discount!

Oh, these local merchants!

Every day they hang out their ready-made clothes and display their fabrics and goods in the windows; but seldom is anyone seen entering their doors. I guessed at the outset there must be the odd peasant-farmer from up the valley, coming to town on business; and I guessed correctly. Today I saw that farmer—and what splendid entertainment he provided!

He was dressed like the peasants in our folktales, in a short knitted jacket with silver buttons, and gray trousers patched with black leather behind. He was driving a tiny little hay wagon with a tiny little horse; in the wagon stood a little red flanked cow, doubtless en route for the butcher. All three—man, horse, and cow—were so diminutive and Paleolithic as to resemble subterranean gnomes on a brief visit to the haunts of men; I was expecting to see them vanish before my eyes. Suddenly the cow let out a bellow from its Lilliputian carriage; and even this preposterous sound came as if from another world.

Some two hours later I saw the man again, without his horse or cow, wandering around the stores on his errands. I followed him into the emporium of one Vogt:

Saddler, Glazier, and (for good measure) Leather Merchant. This versatile man of commerce wanted to serve me first; but I said I needed to look at a saddle and some glass and a sample of leather first; no hurry where I was concerned. The merchant then turned to the gnome.

The two were acquainted.

"Well, if it isn't himself back in town!"

"Ay, that's about long and short on't."

The whole gamut: the weather, the wind, the state of the roads; the wife, the kids (much the same as usual); the crops; the river (fallen by a quarter this last week); the price of meat; the hard times we're living in. Then they started in on the leather: feeling it, turning it, bending it, talking it over. And when at last a strip had been cut and weighed, the gnome thought it must be bewitched and all to weigh so much. Best reckon in round sums—no sense in fiddle-faddling with all them bits and pieces of weight. On this issue they racked their brains for a while, as form and custom prescribe. When finally the moment for paying arrived, a leather purse was conjured up as if from a fairy tale, one by one the prehistoric coins were solemnly and gingerly fished out, both parties counted them again and again, and the gnome closed the purse with an anxious movement: that was all he had!

"But you've paper money too, as well as change? Didn't I see a bank note?"

"Bank note? Nay, I'm not breaking into *him*."

More racking of brains, prolonged discussion, a little give-and-take on both sides—and the deal was done.

"That was a cruelly dear piece of leather," said the purchaser.

And the seller replied, "No, you got it dirt cheap. Now don't forget to look me up any time you're in town."

Late in the afternoon I saw the gnome driving home again after his visit to the haunts of men. The cow had stayed behind with the butcher. The little man's parcels and sacks were in the wagon, but he himself was plodding along behind, the leather on his backside standing out in a triangle at each step. Whether his wits were naturally weak, or whether they had been over-taxed by a visit to the liquor store, he was wearing a roll of shoe leather around one arm like a bracelet.

And so, once more, money had poured into town: a peasant farmer had been in and sold his cow, and bought himself out of small change again. The event was immediately noted everywhere: even the three lawyers took note, even the three little local newspapers took note—the circulation of money was on the increase. Unproductive activity; and the town lived on it.

Every week, however, town houses were offered for sale in the local papers; every week, the authorities published a numbered list of properties on the tax rolls which were to be sold in liquidation of unpaid tax. Well, what of it? Ah, but the sheer number of houses for sale in this way! The barren mountain valley with its great river could not feed this moribund town; a cow now and again was not enough. Hence the enforced surrender of town houses and Swiss chalets and dwellings of every kind. On the west coast, if once in a while a small town house is up for sale, it's a major event; the natives gather on the mackerel quay, putting their heads together and whispering. Here in our little town, which had lost all hope, it occasioned no remark when a property slipped from an exhausted hand. My turn today, my neighbor's turn tomorrow! And no one to shed a tear.

Engineer Lassen came to my lodgings and said, "Put your cap on and come with me to the station to fetch a trunk."

"No," I answered. "I'm not doing that."

"Not doing that?"

"No. There's a man at the hotel for that. I don't grudge him his earnings."

I had made my point. The engineer was so young,

he could only stare at me in silence. And when, being persistent by nature, he returned to the attack, his tone had changed.

"I'd sooner have you than anyone on this occasion," he said; "and I'm sure you wouldn't mind."

"That's another matter; in that case I'll do it."

I put on my cap and was ready. He led the way to the station; I followed behind. We waited ten minutes, then the train arrived: three little boxlike cars, out of which crawled a handful of passengers. From the last car there crawled a lady; the engineer strode off to assist her.

I took no special notice of what went on. The lady, who was gloved and veiled, handed the engineer a yellow summer coat. She seemed shy and spoke only a few quiet words; but when, by contrast, the engineer talked loudly and freely and begged her to take off her veil, she grew bolder and did as he said. "Do you recognize me now?" she asked. And at once I pricked up my ears—it was Mrs. Falkenberg's voice. I turned and looked her in the face.

How hard it is to be old and superannuated! The moment I realized whom I was standing before, I was concerned only with my own aged person, with my dignity of bearing, with the depth of my bow. I was now the possessor of a tunic and trousers of brown corduroy such as workmen wear in the south—a handsome outfit, and brand new; but alas, I wasn't wearing it that day. How irritated, how downcast this made me! And while they stood there talking, I started to wonder why the engineer had so particularly wanted me to accompany him to the station. To save the tip to the porter, perhaps? To strut around with his own personal servant? Or did he wish to cheer Madame with the sight of a familiar face? If so, the idea was sadly misconceived; the moment she saw me, Madame went rigid with displeasure at finding me here, where she might have fancied herself well hidden. I heard the engineer say, "See this fellow here? He'll take your trunk. Got the ticket?" But I gave no sign of greeting and turned away.

Afterward I stood gloating over him in my miserable soul, and thinking: Ah, now she will take against him for his tactlessness! He has presented for her inspection a man who has been in her employment when she had a home; but that same man had a sense of delicacy, he turned away without recognizing her! (And God alone knew why the ladies ran after this kid, with his concave back and enormous bottom.)

There were fewer and fewer people on the platform; the train's crew uncoupled the three little boxes and began forming them into another train; in the end we were the only people left. The engineer and Madame still stood there talking. Why had she come? Search me! The young firebrand must have missed her and wanted to have her again. Or perhaps she had come of her own free will, to explain the lie of the land and seek his advice. Sooner or later, no doubt, it would end in their getting engaged and then married. Mr. Hugo Lassen was a knight-at-arms, of course, and she his beloved here on earth. It only remained to be seen if her path would be strewn with happiness and flowers ever after.

"No, that won't do at all!" exclaimed the engineer, laughing. "If you won't be my aunt, then you'll have to be my cousin."

"Sh!" she answered. "Can't that man go away?"

Whereupon the engineer came up to me with the luggage ticket in his hand and said, in the lordly manner of an Inspector of Log Driving addressing his team, "Bring the trunk up to the hotel."

"Very good," I answered, touching my cap.

As I carried the trunk I thought: So now he's asking her to be his aunt, his elderly aunt! Again, he could have been more tactful—as I would have been. I would have said to all and sundry, "There is come a fair angel unto King Hugo. Behold how young she is and how comely. Her gray eyes tell of a heavy heart; yea, her glance is grave. But a myriad lights shimmer in her hair, and I do love her. Behold her also when she speaks, her mouth is altogether good and delicate; sometimes it cannot choose but yield a smile. I am King Hugo this day, and she is my beloved!"

The trunk was no heavier than many another burden, but it was fitted with bronzed iron bands, one of which tore a hole in the back of my smock. Then I thanked my lucky stars that it wasn't my corduroy tunic which had been ruined.

## VII

Several days passed. I was bored with my futile occupation, which consisted of doing precisely nothing, of idling in fact; and I applied to the log drivers' foreman for a place in his team. But he turned me down.

These lords of the proletariat are tremendous swells; they look down on the farm worker and don't want him anywhere near them. They roam from watercourse to watercourse, live a free and easy life, get cash in their hands once a week, and as likely as not drink most of it away. They are also in good favor with the girls. It's the same with road workers, railroad workers, and factory workers of every kind: they regard even the craftsman as a lower form of being, while as for the farm worker, he is a serf!

By now I felt certain that I could join the gang whenever I chose, by telling the Inspector of Log Driving that I wished to do so. But, in the first place, I had no desire to place myself further in the man's debt; and, in the second place, I would have to be prepared for my worthy colleagues giving me hell—right up until the moment when, with great difficulty, I had earned their respect. And that might take longer than I was prepared to spend.

In any case, the engineer came to me one day with instructions which I was to observe with all possible care. Speaking courteously and reasonably, he said, "There's been no rain for a long time now; the river's falling and the jams are growing. I want you to tell the man higher up and the man lower down to take every possible care at present; I need hardly say that goes for you too."

"There's bound to be rain very soon now," I said, for the sake of saying something.

"Be that as it may," he replied with all the seriousness of youth, "I have to act as if it were never going to rain any more. Now remember every syllable I've said. I can't be everywhere myself, especially now that I've got a visitor."

At this I took him as seriously as he took himself and swore to do my level best.

But this meant I couldn't yet give up my idle life; instead, I continued wandering upstream and downstream with my boat hook and my provisions. For my own satisfaction I took to clearing bigger and bigger jams unaided, singing to myself as if I was an entire team of log drivers, and working as hard as a dozen men. I also conveyed the engineer's instructions to Grindhusen and put the fear of God in him.

But then came the rain.

And now the logs fairly danced down the waterfalls and rapids, like great tawny snakes that darted on and on, with sometimes the heads and sometimes the tails in the air.

Carefree days for the engineer, I presumed.

As for myself, I disliked both the town and my boardinghouse; I had my own little room, but took no pleasure in it, since it let in every sound in the place. Besides, my nose was put well and truly out of joint by all the young log men who lodged there. At this period I paced the riverbank assiduously, even though there was little or nothing for me to do. At times, however, I would steal away to a hiding place under a cliff, where I would sit feeling old and forsaken, and wallowing in the sensation. And in the evenings I would write letter after letter to my acquaintances as a way of talking to them; but I never posted the letters. In short, these were cheerless days. The greatest pleasure I had was to crisscross my way through the town, observing trivial things and reflecting a little on each.

But was the engineer still so carefree? I began to have my doubts.

Why was he no longer out in the streets early and late with the visiting cousin? He was even capable of stopping another young lady on the bridge and asking about her health—something he had not done these last two weeks. Once or twice I had seen him with Mrs. Falkenberg; she looked young and chic and happy, even a trifle wild—she laughed aloud. That's what it means, I thought, to be a newly compromised woman; but to-morrow or the day after it may be different. The next time I saw her I was irked by the frivolity that I found both in her clothes and in her nature; she had lost some of her former appeal, her sweetness. What had become of the tenderness in her gaze? Now there was only boldness. I said to myself in a fury: That's what her eyes are like—the two flickering lights at the entrance to a cabaret show.

But then it seemed as if they had started to weary of each other's company, since the engineer increasingly went about on his own, leaving Mrs. Falkenberg to sit at her window in the hotel, gazing out. This, perhaps, was why fat Captain Brother now reappeared on the scene; his high spirits and capacity for enjoyment were to infect others than himself. And the monstrously misshapen companion of mirth certainly did his best. One whole night through the little town rang with his roguish laughter; then his leave ran out and he had to rejoin his regiment. The engineer and Mrs. Falkenberg were left on their own once more.

One day, while standing in a shop, I heard that Engineer Lassen had had some slight disagreement with his cousin. Or so a traveling salesman reported to the storekeeper. But such was the respect in which the wealthy engineer was held in our town that the storekeeper would scarcely believe his ears. With an incredulous air he said to the tattletale, "It must have been a joke between them. Did you hear them yourself? When was it?"

And now the salesman did not dare to make too much of his tale.

"My room's right next to the engineer's," he said, "so I couldn't help hearing what went on last night. No doubt about it: they were arguing. Mind you, I'm not saying it was anything very much; quite the opposite, the merest bagatelle. All she said was that he was different from before, he'd changed, and he answered by saying he didn't dare do as he'd like, not in this town. Then she asked him to dismiss some man she'd taken against, one of the log drivers, I guess. And he said he would."

"Well, that's nothing at all," said the storekeeper.

But the traveling salesman looked as if he had certainly heard more than he chose to come out with now.

And had I not noticed myself how the engineer had changed? The man who had spoken so loudly and happily that first day at the station was now given to stubborn silences on the rare occasions when he walked with Madame on the bridge; I saw them both, just standing there, staring in different directions. God in heaven, love is a volatile substance!

At first all was well. Doubtless she said something like, "How lovely it is to be here; the river is so big, and the torrent so swift, and its roar so strange; and here is a little town with streets and people, and here are you!" And he answered, "Yes, and here are you!" And each was peerless in the other's eyes. But soon they were sated with pleasure, they drove it too hard, they fashioned love to an article measured by the ell, such fools they were. The conviction grew on him that things had taken a wrong turning; the town was so small, his cousin a stranger there; he could not go on being her constant cavalier, they must tear themselves away from each other a little, must perhaps occasionally—just once in a while, you understand! eat at different times at the hotel's board. Otherwise those traveling salesmen would start putting two and two together about this pair of cousins. For remember, it's a small town! And she—how incapable she was of understanding this! Surely the town was no smaller now than at first? No, my darling, it is you who have changed!

We now had abundant rain, and the work went at a rattling pace. Yet the engineer had started taking little trips up and down the river. It seemed as if he wanted, above all, to get away from home. His face, too, was deeply careworn these days.

One day he asked me to go up to Grindhusen and fetch him down to the office. Was it Grindhusen, per-haps, who was about to be dismissed? But Madame had never even set eyes on Grindhusen since she ar-rived; what could he have done to her?

I fetched Grindhusen to the town, where he re-ported at once to the engineer. The latter put on his hat and coat, and off they went together; they set out up the river and were soon out of sight.

Later that day Grindhusen came to my boarding-house, clearly eager to talk; but I asked him no ques-tions. In the evening he got some brandy from the log drivers and began to open up. What kind of cousin was this that the Inspector of Log Driving had got hold of? Wasn't she due to be on her way again shortly? No one knew the answer to that—why should she be on her way again? "It's nothing but everlasting monkey business and ruination with these cousins," Grindhusen declared. "He'd do much better to find himself a girl he could marry—and what's more, I told him so." "Go on, you didn't!" someone else said. "I did, you know," said Grindhusen, pleased as Punch with himself; "there I was, sitting talking to the inspector just like he was one of you. Why do you suppose he sent for me? You'll never guess, not if you sit there till the cows come home. He sent for me, let me tell you, so he could conversate with me. Just so as he could conversate with me. Not but what he hasn't done so before, only it's this time I'm referring to." "What did he talk to you about?" someone asked. Grindhusen puffed and preened. "Now, look here, I'm not so dumb that I don't know how to talk to a man. And I'm not what you'd call a contradictions type either, as far as I'm aware. 'Grindhusen,' the inspector says to me; 'you know a thing or two, you do,' he says; 'here's two kroner for you.' Those were his very words. And if you don't believe me, you can see the two-krone piece. There it is!" "Yes, but what did you *talk* about?"

shouted several voices at once. "I don't think he ought to tell us," I said.

It occurred to me that the inspector must have been in a state of torture and despair when he sent me to fetch Grindhusen. He was so little versed in the world that the moment anything went wrong he felt the need of someone to confide in. At present he was going around day after day feeling sorry for himself, with a long face as if to let the world know of the sorrow that God had laid on him in interrupting his fun and games. This sportsman with the protruding bottom was a mere travesty of young manhood, a sniveling Spartan. What sort of upbringing had he had?

Ah, but had the engineer been old, I would have found excuses for him in plenty; maybe I only hated him for being young. Who could say? All the same, he struck me as a travesty.

When I had said my little say, Grindhusen stared at me, and all the others stared at me.

"Well, perhaps I shouldn't really tell you," said Grindhusen, vacillating.

But the log drivers protested, "Why shouldn't he tell us? We'd never dream of spreading it any further."

"Certainly not," said another. "But maybe *you're* one of those who go in for mailing poison-pen letters to the inspector."

Whereupon Grindhusen too plucked up courage and said, "I'll say what I like, don't you worry! I'll tell you just as much as I choose. Yes. Because I'm not saying anything but what's the honest truth. And if you really want to know, the inspector will be coming any day now and giving *you* a small item of news. That's what he'll be doing, according to my information. So you don't need to bother yourself. And with regard to anything I choose to tell you about this, that, or the other, I'm telling you no more than what's the honest truth. So put that in your pipe. Yes. And if you knew what I know, you'd know that she's nothing but an aggravation and a scandal to the inspector, and he can't go out in the town because of her. Cousin indeed!"

"All right, all right," said the log drivers, trying to calm him.

"Why do you suppose he sent for me? Yes, there sits the guy who brought the message! But he'll be getting a message himself one of these days, if I understand the inspector correctly. I say no more. And with regard to anything I choose to tell you, why, he's been like a father to me, and I'd need to have a heart of stone to say any different. He says to me, 'I'm so depressed and miserable all day—do you know a cure for that, Grindhusen?' 'No,' I says, 'but the inspector himself knows one,' I says. Those were my very words. 'I don't know about that,' he says, 'but it's these wretched females,' he says. 'Ah,' I says, 'if it's females, they're a regular pain in the neck.' 'You're dead right there,' he says. 'But,' I says, 'it strikes me the inspector can take them and do his bit with them, and then give them a couple of good hard raps over the tailbone,' I says. 'By God, I believe you're right there too, Grindhusen,' says the inspector, cheering up no end. I've never seen anyone cheer up so quickly and get right back on top again, just for a word or two. It was quite something to see, I can tell you. Stone me if it isn't gospel truth, every syllable I've told you. I sat there just like I'm sitting here now, see, and the inspector, he sat like it might be *there*…''

Grindhusen maundered on and on.

Next morning, before it was properly light, I was stopped in the street by Engineer Lassen. It was only half past three.

I stood there with my boat hook and rations, fully armed for a march upriver. Grindhusen had embarked on a drinking bout in town, and my plan was to cover his district as well, then continue right to the watershed. For this reason I had double rations in my knapsack.

The engineer, it was obvious, had come from a party:

he was laughing and talking loudly with two other men—all of them the worse for drink.

"Go on ahead!" he told the others. Then he turned to me and asked, "Where are you off to?"

I explained my plans to him.

"Hm, I'm not so sure about that," he said. "No, it's not worth it—surely Grindhusen can manage. Besides, I'm about to make a tour of inspection myself. What do you mean by planning a trip like this without saying a word to me about it?"

He was right enough; and I apologized. Indeed, I ought to have had more sense—knowing how much he liked being the boss and ordering us about.

But my apology had merely given him the taste of blood. His righteous anger boiled over, and he said, "I won't have this kind of thing. My workers are here to do as I tell them, period. I took you on because I wanted to help you, not because I needed you—and anyway, I don't need you any longer."

I just stood there, staring at him.

"You can come to my office later today and collect your wages," he added, turning as if to go.

So I was the one to be dismissed! Now I understood Grindhusen's veiled allusions. Mrs. Falkenberg must have found she couldn't stand the sight of me here, reminding her of home, and had arranged for me to be sent packing. But surely I, and I alone, had shown a sense of delicacy toward her at the station, turning away instead of recognizing her. And had I ever once paid her any mark of attention on meeting her in the street? Didn't one display of delicacy deserve another?

And now here was this young engineer dismissing me with exaggerated anger. How well I fancied I understood him! For days he had been shrinking from this task; finally he had managed it, after a whole night spent in drinking his way to courage. Was I doing him an injustice? Perhaps; and I fought against my own reasoning. I reminded myself again that he was young, while I was old and probably eaten up with envy on that account. So I refrained from sarcasm and simply said in reply, "Ah well, in that case I'd better empty my knapsack again."

But the engineer evidently wanted to strike again while the iron was still hot, and reminded me about the incident of the trunk.

"And when I get a flat no after giving an order," he said, "I don't find it funny at all. I'm not used to that. And since I can't be certain it won't happen again, it's best if you go."

"Yes, all right," I said.

At the window of the hotel I glimpsed a figure in white, and guessed it was Mrs. Falkenberg who stood there watching us. So I made no more ado.

But then the engineer seemed suddenly to remember that he couldn't quite get rid of me here and now: he still had to pay me, we were bound to meet once more. So he changed his tone and said, "Well—come sometime during the day and collect your wages. Have you thought about what you should have?"

"No. That's for the engineer to decide."

"Well, well," he said, mollified. "All in all, you've been a good man to have around, I can't deny it. But various circumstances—besides, it's not just my idea, you know how these females—I mean ladies…"

Yes, indeed—he was young all right. And denied himself nothing.

"Well—good day!"—and with an abrupt nod he was gone.


But the day proved too short for me: I wandered into the forest, and stayed there so long on my own that I never got to the office for my wages. Not that there was any hurry; I had plenty of time.

What should I do now?

I had no great affection for our little town; but I had begun to find it more interesting and could have wished to remain there yet awhile. Certain complications were arising between two people whose fortunes I had followed closely for some weeks; at any moment now some further development might occur—who could tell? To avoid leaving town, I toyed with the idea of becoming a blacksmith's apprentice; but for one thing the work would have tied me to the smithy all day and generally restricted my movements, while, for another, the apprenticeship would have taken too many years of my life. And years were the very article I was now so short of.

So I let the days go by, one after another; they were warm and sunny days once more. I lived in the same lodgings, mended my clothes, and had some new ones made at a store. One of the servants at the boarding-house came one evening and offered to do my mending; but I was in a joking mood, and showed her instead how well I could fend for myself: look at this patch, and look at that one! After a while a man came up the stairs and began rattling my door and saying, "Open up there!" "It's Henrik, one of the log men," said the girl. "Is he your sweetheart?" I asked. "Lord, no!" she answered; "I'd sooner go without than have someone like him." "Open up, I tell you!" shouted the man in the corridor. But the girl said boldly, "Let him go on standing there!" So we did—though at times my door buckled visibly under his more furious assaults.

When we had run out of jokes about my patches and her sweethearts, I had to reconnoiter the corridor before the girl would venture out. But the man had gone.

It was now late in the evening. I went down to the parlor, where Grindhusen was drinking with some of the log drivers. "That's him!" called out one of them—Henrik, no doubt—as I entered. He at once started egging on his mates; and even Grindhusen ganged up with the others in trying to bait me.

Poor Grindhusen! He went around nowadays with a permanent hangover, which he couldn't shake off. He had had yet another conference with Engineer Lassen; they had wandered away upstream as before and sat talking for an hour; on his return Grindhusen produced another two-krone piece he'd been given. And again he had got drunk and blustered away about being the engineer's confidant. Tonight, too, he was as high and mighty as a polar explorer who has wintered in the Arctic; he wouldn't crawl, not even to the king.

"Come and sit down," he said to me.

I sat down.

But one or two of the log drivers objected to my company, and as soon as Grindhusen became aware of this, he swung right around and set about teasing me and committing further indiscretions about the engineer and his cousin.

"Well, have you been fired?" he asked, with a wink at the others as if to command their attention.

"Yes," I said.

"Really? Well, I knew that weeks ago, but I never said a word. I don't mind saying that I knew before anyone in the whole world of us here, but did I utter a single squeak? The inspector, he says, 'I want your advice, Grindhusen,' he says; 'it's about whether you'd fancy being down here in the town for a while instead of the other man who I'm going to fire,' he says. 'As far as that's concerned,' I says, 'it all depends on what the inspector commands.' Those were my very words, down to the last syllable. But did I utter a single squeak?"

"*Have* you been fired?" one of the log drivers asked.

"Yes," I said.

"As for that cousin," Grindhusen continued, "the inspector asked me about her, too. Wants my advice about every blessed thing, he does. And this last time we were upriver together, he sort of slapped his knee at the thought of her. Yes. Well, you can go on guessing till the cows come home. Posh food and drink she has to have, and posh everything—it's costing a fortune every week; and still she doesn't go. Shit! That's what I say—I don't believe in mincing words."

But now my dismissal seemed to be working in my favor; some of the men may have felt sorry for me, while others, no doubt, were glad I'd been sent packing. One offered me some of his brandy, and called to the maid for a glass—and mind it's properly clean! Even Henrik forgot his grudge and clinked glasses with me. And we sat for a long while idling away the time.

"Only don't forget to go for your money," Grindhusen advised me. "Because the inspector's got no intention of bringing it to you, according to my information. 'There's some money for him sitting in my office,' says the inspector; 'but perhaps he expects me to come and hand it to him on a platter,' he says."

## VIII

In the event, the engineer was not so far from handing me the money on a platter. However, it was an unsought victory and a meaningless one.

The engineer called on me at my lodgings and said, "Would you come with me, please, and collect your money? There's a letter for you, too; it came in the post."

We went up to the engineer's office—and there was Mrs. Falkenberg. I was greatly surprised, but bowed and remained standing near the door.

"Do sit down, please," said the engineer. He went to his desk and found my letter. "Here you are. No, do please sit and read it here; I'll just be working out your pay in the meanwhile. "

And even Mrs. Falkenberg motioned me to a chair.

Why did they both look so tense? Why all this sudden politeness and "please" every other word? The explanation was not long in coming: the letter was from Captain Falkenberg.

"Do you want to borrow this?" asked Madame, handing me a paper knife.

A short, friendly letter, and nothing more; the opening even mildly jocular:

I had left Øvrebø before he knew I was going; what was more, I had left without my pay. If I had got the impression that he was in difficulties and unable to pay me until harvest time and that was the reason for my sudden departure, then he hoped I would realize I had been mistaken. And now he wished very much that I would come back as soon as possible unless I was committed elsewhere. He wanted to have all the various buildings painted, then there would be the harvest, and finally he would value my help in felling timber. "It all looks lovely here now—crops growing tall and grass growing fat! Please let me have an answer to this letter as soon as possible. Kind regards, Captain Falkenberg."

The engineer finished his calculations, turned sideways in his chair, and gazed at the wall; then, as if he had hit on something, he turned quickly back to the desk again. Pure nervousness. Madame stood looking at her rings; but I sensed that she had been observing me on the sly throughout. How frightened they both were!

Then the engineer said, "Oh, by the way, I see your letter's from Captain Falkenberg. How are things with him? I know his handwriting, of course."

"Would you like to read it?" I said at once, offering it to him. What harm could there be?

"No. No, thank you, I didn't mean that. It was just…"

All the same, he took the letter. And Madame went up to him and looked over his shoulder as he read.

"Uh-huh," said the engineer, nodding. "Yes, everything seems to be all right. Thanks." And he held out the letter to give it back.

But Madame chose to interpret his movement another way; she seized the letter and began perusing it for herself. The paper shook slightly in her hand.

"Now, how about settling up?" said the engineer.

"Here you are—your money. I don't know whether you feel that's enough ?"

"Yes, thank you," I answered.

The engineer seemed relieved to find that Captain Falkenberg's letter concerned me and no one else. He made another attempt to play down my dismissal, saying, "Well, well. If you ever come this way again, you know where you can find me. The log driving's finished for this year in any case—the weather's been so dry lately."

Madame stood there, reading. Then she was reading no longer—her eyes never moved—but merely staring at the letter, lost in thought. What was she thinking about?

The engineer glanced at her impatiently and said with a half smile, "My dear, you surely don't need to learn that letter by heart! Can't you see the man's waiting for it?"

"I'm sorry," said Madame; and she handed me the letter with a quick, embarrassed movement. "I was forgetting myself."

"Evidently," said the engineer.

I bowed and left.

On summer evenings the bridge was thick with promenaders: teachers and merchants, teenage girls and children. I would wait until the evening was far advanced and the bridge deserted; then I too would stroll out there and station myself in the midst of the roar for an hour or so. Why do anything but listen? However, my brain was so well rested, with all my idleness and good sound sleep, that it found innumerable things to busy itself with. The evening before, I had decided in all seriousness to go to Mrs. Falkenberg and say, "Take the first train, Madame, and go!" Today I had laughed at myself over this idiotic idea and exchanged it for another: Take the first train yourself, my dear sir, and go! Are you her peer and counselor? No, indeed; and what one does must not be hopelessly at odds with what one is!

That evening I continued to treat myself according to my deserts. I started to hum, but could scarcely hear my own humming; it was roared to death by the torrent. "You should always stand over a torrent when you want to hum," I told myself in cutting tones; then I laughed at myself. Such were the childish fancies with which I frittered away the time.

An inland torrent does to the ear what ocean breakers do. But a breaker surges forward, now strongly, now feebly, whereas the roar of a torrent is like an audible fog, absurd in its monotonousness, totally lacking in reason, a miracle of idiocy. What's the time? No, not at all! Is it day or night? Yes! Like laying a stone across twelve keys of an organ, then going away.

Such were the childish fancies with which I frittered away the time.

"Good evening!" said Mrs. Falkenberg at my elbow.

I wasn't greatly surprised; I suppose I had been expecting her. After her performance with her husband's letter, she might well proceed further.

There seemed to be two ways of viewing Madame's appearance: either she had turned sweet and sentimental at being so directly reminded of her home, or she wanted to make the engineer jealous; he might at that very moment be watching us from his window—and I had been summoned back to Øvrebø. For that matter, it was on the books that yesterday too she had been practicing her wiles, trying to make the engineer jealous by studying the Captain's letter so intently.

But neither of my flashes of insight, it seemed, was going to be confirmed. It was on my account that she had come—merely to apologize, after a fashion, for getting me dismissed. A bagatelle like that should have left her completely indifferent! Was she so utterly frivolous as not to appreciate the dismal nature of her own present position? Why the hell should she concern herself over mine?

I thought of saying a few terse words and pointing toward the train; instead, I found myself being gentle with her, as with someone not fully responsible, a child.

"So now I suppose you're off to Øvrebø?" she said. "If so, I'd like to…Hm. It's a bad business for you, I dare say, having to leave—yes? No? No, no. But there's something you don't know: it was I who got you dismissed."

"It doesn't matter."

"No, no. But just to let you know. And now that you're going back to Øvrebø, I suppose, I wanted to tell you. You can understand it was a bit embarrassing for me to…"

She broke off.

"To have me around. Yes, it would be embarrassing."

"To keep seeing you. I mean, just a bit embarrassing. Because, of course, you knew where I came from. So I asked the engineer if he couldn't fire you. Not that he wanted to, of course—but in the end he did. I'm glad you're going to Øvrebø."

I said, "Really? But when Madame comes home again, won't it be just as embarrassing to see me there?"

"Home?" she said. "I'm not going there."

Pause. She had knitted her brows as she spoke. But

then she nodded, even smiled a little, and started to go.

"Well, you'll forgive me, then," she said.

"Do you mind at all my going back to the Captain?" I asked.

She stopped and looked me full in the face. How to read her mind correctly? Three times she had mentioned Øvrebø; was she figuring that I might let slip a good word for her when I got there? Or was she afraid of being indebted to me for the favor of my *not* going?

"No, no, I don't mind," she answered. "Go, by all means."

Then she walked away.

She had been neither sentimental nor calculating, as far as I could see. Or again, she might well have been both. And what had I to show for my attempt to gain her confidence? I ought to have known better than to try. Whether she was here or elsewhere was no business of mine. Her pigeon!

I said to myself: You're all agog, aren't you? You kid yourself that she's merely literature to you—yet that wizened soul of yours puts out fresh shoots the moment she is friendly toward you and starts looking at you with those eyes of hers. You fill me with shame and grief, and tomorrow you're going!

Only I didn't go.

But it was true that I was all agog, all ears, for news of Mrs. Falkenberg; and equally true that many a night I took myself to task on this account, and tortured myself with self-contempt. From early morn till night I thought of her: Is she up? Has she slept well? Is she going back home today? And at the same time my head was full of schemes: I might get work for a while at the hotel where she was staying. Or I could write home for some clothes, turn gentleman myself, and stay at that same hotel. This last idea would at once have cut the ground from under my feet, and left me further removed from her than ever; yet it was one that I particularly favored—I had no more sense than that. I had been cultivating the friendship of the underporter at the hotel, purely and simply because he lived nearer to her than I did. He was a big, strong fellow who used to meet the trains; and once every two weeks he would collect a salesman coming to display his wares in the hotel room dedicated to this purpose. He never had any news for me; I neither questioned him directly nor tried to manipulate him into saying something of his own accord; besides, he was not strong in the head. But he lived under the same roof as Madame—ah, that he did! And one day this acquaintanceship of ours led to my learning a great and good piece of news about Mrs. Falkenberg—and from her own lips.

So not all days in that little town were equally unpleasant.

One day I accompanied the underporter back from the station, where he had met the morning train and collected a salesman of some substance—the horse and cart were needed for his heavy gray trunks.

I had helped him with some lifting at the station; now, back at the hotel, he looked at me and said, "You could do me a favor helping get these trunks in—and I'll buy you a beer this evening."

So we carried the trunks in together; they were needed at once in the display room on the second floor, where the salesman was waiting for them. It was no problem for two big, strong fellows like us.

When there was only one trunk left in the cart, the underporter was detained for a moment in the display room by the traveler's giving him some errand or other to run. Meanwhile, I stood waiting for him in the corridor; I was a stranger here and didn't care to slink off down the stairs on my own.

At that moment Engineer Lassen's office door opened, and he and Mrs. Falkenberg came out. They looked as if they had only just got up; they were bareheaded, and doubtless on their way to the breakfast table. Whether they failed to see me standing there, or whether perhaps they took me for the underporter, they continued their conversation. He was saying, "Quite so. And it's not going to change. I simply don't understand why you should feel so lonely."

"You understand very well," she retorted.

"I do not. And I think you should make an effort to be more cheerful."

"You think nothing of the kind. You prefer me to stay like this—heartbroken because you don't want me any more."

"Are you crazy?" he asked, stopping at the head of the stairs.

"Yes, I think I must be," she answered.

Which was a fairly feeble thing to say; but then she always got the worst of a quarrel. Why could she not exert herself to find some wounding, deadly reply?

He ran his hand along the banister and said, "So you think I enjoy this state of affairs? I can't tell you the torture it is. And it's been torture to me for a long time."

"And for me too. But now I'm going to put an end to it."

"Really. You've said that before—you said it last week, in fact."

"Yes, but this time I'm leaving."

He looked up. "You're leaving?"

"Yes, very soon."

But then he must have wanted to gloss over the eagerness, the positive joy, with which he had jumped at her words. He said, "Nonsense, you're going to be a nice, cheerful cousin, and then you won't have to leave."

"No, this time I'm leaving," she said, passing him and going down the stairs.

He followed.

Then the underporter came out and we went down together. The last trunk was smaller than the others, and I asked him to carry it up on his own, pretending I had hurt my hand. I helped him lift the trunk onto his back and went home. Now I could leave in the morning.

Late that afternoon Grindhusen, too, was dismissed. The engineer had sent for him and given him a dressing down for doing no work, but loafing around the town, getting drunk; now he didn't need him any longer.

I reflected on the astonishing speed with which the engineer had gained new courage. He was so young, he had needed this man to comfort him and say yea to his every word; but now that a certain tiresome cousin would soon be on her way, he no longer needed comfort. Or was my aged soul doing him an injustice?

Grindhusen was deeply dejected. He had counted on remaining in this town the whole summer, as the inspector's odd-job man; now that hope had collapsed in ruins. No, the Inspector of Log Driving was no longer like a father to him; and Grindhusen took his disappointment very hard. In paying him off the inspector had wanted to deduct the two-krone pieces which he had given Grindhusen at different times, maintaining that they had only been meant as an advance. Grindhusen sat in the parlor telling us all about this, and adding that the inspector paid meanly enough in any case. At this someone laughed and said, "But did he do like he'd threatened? He didn't, did he?"

"No," answered Grindhusen, "he didn't dare knock off more than the one."

There was general laughter at this, and some wag asked, "Was it the first or the second two-kroner he knocked off? Haha-ha-ha, that's the funniest thing I've ever heard!"

But Grindhusen didn't laugh; he only fretted more and more. What should he do now? All the seasonal jobs had gone by this time, and here he was. He asked me where I was going and, when I told him, begged me to put in a word for him with Captain Falkenberg about his working there for the summer. Meanwhile, he would stay on in the town and wait till he heard from me.

But what would become of Grindhusen's money if

he stayed on in the town? It seemed best to take him along with me; and this I did. Among other things, he had once been a demon for painting, had my mate Grindhusen; had I not watched him paint old Gunhild's cottage on the island? Now he could give me a hand. And later, no doubt, a solution would be found; there must be all kinds of seasonal work on the Captain's estate to keep him going throughout the summer.

The sixteenth of July saw me at Øvrebø once more. I remember dates better and better, partly because I am older, so that the interest which the senile take in dates has been sharpened, partly because as a worker I have to keep track of my working days. But while the old man remembers his dates, he cheerfully forgets more important things. Until now I have forgotten to mention that my letter from Captain Falkenberg had been addressed to me care of Engineer Lassen. Well, it had. And this had immediately struck me as significant: it meant that the Captain was aware of whom I was working for. And I thought to myself at the time, Perhaps the Captain knows who else has been care of Engineer Lassen this summer!

The Captain was still away with his regiment and was not expected home for another week; but Grindhusen got a good reception nonetheless. Nils was delighted that I had brought my mate with me; but, instead of handing him over to me to help with the painting, he sent him on his own responsibility to work in the potato and turnip fields, where there was any amount of weeding and thinning out to be done. Nils himself was well on with the haying.

He was the same blissfully dedicated farmer as ever. At the first break, while the horses were feeding, he took me out and showed me the cornfields and the meadows. Everything was fine; but spring had been late that year, so the timothy was only just beginning to form spikes and the clover to flower. During the recent rain, part of the first year's crop had been flattened too badly to rise again, so Nils had set to work on it with the reaper.

We returned home through billowing grass and corn; there was a rustling in the winter rye and the fat six-rowed barley, reminding Nils of a lovely line of Bjørnson's he had learned at school: *Begynder som en susen i kornet sommerdag*—"Beginning like a whisper in the corn one summer day."

"No—it's time I was taking the horses out again," said Nils, lengthening his stride. Then, with a final sweeping gesture toward the fields, he added, "What a harvest we shall have if only we can get it safely in!"

So Grindhusen went to work in the fields, while I

started on the painting. I began with the barn, and everything that was to be red; then I primed the flagpole and the summerhouse with oil. The house itself I wanted to save till the end. It was built in good, traditional manor-house style, with massive, richly ornamented eaves and a carved Grecian border over the main entrance. At present the house was yellow, and a fresh supply of yellow paint had arrived; but I took it upon myself to send this paint back and get it exchanged. In my view the house should be stone-gray, with doors and windows and gableboards picked out in white. But the Captain would have to decide.

Though everyone in the place was as nice as could be, the cook mild in her authority and Ragnhild as bright-eyed as ever, we all missed the master and mistress. Only the worthy Grindhusen missed no one and nothing. With regular work and good food he grew fat and contented within a matter of days. His only worry was that the Captain would dismiss him when he arrived.

But no: Grindhusen was allowed to stay.

# IX

The Captain arrived.

I was giving the barn its second coat of paint; on hearing his voice I descended the ladder. He bade me welcome back.

"Leaving without your money, you!" he said. And I thought he had a suspicious look in his eye as he asked, "Why?"

I answered, briefly and coldly, that I had had no intention of doing the Captain a kindness. My money could wait for me here.

At this he brightened and said, "But of course. Well, I'm very glad you've come. So you think the flagpole should be white?"

Not daring to reveal at once the full extent of what I proposed should be white, I answered only, "Yes. And I've laid in some white paint."

"Have you? Good. You have a companion with you, I hear."

"Yes. But that's for the Captain to decide."

"He can stay. In fact, Nils has already set him to work in the fields. You all do just as you like with me, in any case," he added as a joke. "You've been on the log driving since I saw you last?"

"Yes."

"Hardly the thing for you, was it?" But then, as if afraid of appearing to cross-examine me about my work with the engineer, he changed the subject completely and said, "When are you starting on the house itself?"

"This afternoon, I thought. I need to do some scraping here and there first."

"Fine. While you're at it, put in a nail any place where the board siding's loose. Have you been out in the fields?"

"Yes."

"They look good. You chaps did a fine job in the spring. Now we could do with some rain for the upper fields."

"Grindhusen and I came past lots of places in worse need of rain than the Captain's land. Here we're on clay, even high up on the hills."

"True enough. How did you know that, by the way?"

"I looked around a bit when I was here in the spring," I answered. "And I did a bit of digging here and there. I was thinking that sooner or later the Captain would want to have a water pipe down to the house, so I was looking for water."

"A water pipe? Why, yes, I thought of it at one time, but... Yes, in fact I looked into it a few years ago. But I wasn't able to do it all at one go, and then something or other got in the way. And the money I get from this harvest is needed for other purposes."

A wrinkle appeared for a moment between his eyes; he stood looking down, thinking.

"Still, with the thousand dozen battens I should manage and to spare," he said suddenly. "Water pipe? It would need to go to the house *and* the outbuildings— a regular network, eh?"

"But you'll have no rock to blast your way through."

"Really? Well, we'll have to see. By the way, did you like it in the town? It's not much of a town, but there's more people there, of course. And the odd visitor arriving by train."

Aha, I thought; he certainly knows who's been visiting Engineer Lassen this summer. I answered, truthfully, that I hadn't much cared for the town.

"No? I see."

And as if this had given him food for thought, he gazed into the distance, whistling softly to himself. Then he walked away.

He was in good spirits, and more communicative than I had known him; he nodded to me as he went off. I recognized him from of old: brisk and decided, full of interest in his affairs once more, and sober as a judge. The sight of him put new heart in me as well. Here was no defeated man: for a time he had kept open house for foolishness and debauch, but his own resolution would put an end to that. An oar in the water appears to be broken; but it is whole.

Then the rain set in, and I had to abandon my painting. Nils had been lucky enough to get in all the hay he had cut. Now we were all employed, men and women alike, in weeding the potatoes.

Meanwhile, the Captain stayed indoors, striking an occasional note on Madame's piano, from loneliness and boredom. Now and again he came out to us in the fields, with no umbrella either, letting himself get soaked. "Splendid weather for the soil, eh?" he would say; or, "Looks like being a bumper year." But when he went back home, it was back to himself and his loneliness. As Nils said, "We're better off than he is."

So we weeded the potatoes, and when we had finished with them too, the rain started easing off. Ideal weather, bumper year! Both Nils and I were as proud and contented as if we owned Øvrebø.

And now the haying began in earnest, with the girls out following the machine and spreading the cut hay, and Grindhusen scything wherever the ground was too rough for the machi go. Meanwhile, I coated the house with stone-gray paint.

The Captain came and asked, "What kind of paint's you're using?"

How should I answer? My solution was rather cowardly, but what I feared most was the Captain's forbidding me outright to paint the house gray. I said, "Oh, it's just some paint—I don't know—it's all the same what color we use for the undercoat…"

At least I gained a reprieve: the Captain said no more.

When I had coated the house gray, and the doors and gableboards white, I went down to the summerhouse and painted that the same way. But the resulting color was hideous—the yellow paint showed through and made all the buildings look sallow. The flagpole I took down and painted white all over. Then I spent a few more days with Nils, helping him harvest the hay. We were now in August.

By the time I set to work on the house again, I had conceived the idea of starting so early one morning that I would be far advanced with the painting before the Captain was up—irrevocably far, so to speak. I started at three in the morning; there had been a fall of dew, and I had to rub the walls down with a sack. I worked until four, had some coffee, then on again till eight, which I knew was the Captain's hour for rising; then I went off and helped Nils for an hour. I had reached my target with the painting, and my idea was to give the Captain time to recover from my stone-gray paint, in case he should have got out of bed on the wrong side.

After breakfast I climbed the ladder again and continued painting, all industry and innocence. Up came the Captain.

"Are you putting on a second coat of gray?" he called up to me.

"Good morning! Ye-es. But I don't know—"

"Look, what the hell is going on? Come down off that ladder!"

I came down. But I had completely lost my timidity: I had thought of a sentence which might perhaps do the trick when the moment came. Or had my instinct led me wildly astray?

I began by trying to maintain that it made virtually no difference what color we used for this second coat either; but the Captain cut me short, "Nonsense! Put yellow on top of that gray of yours and the whole thing will be one filthy mess can't you see that?"

"Then perhaps we could finish off with two coats of yellow?"

"Four coats? No! And look at all that zinc white you're squandering! It's far more expensive than the ocher."

He was right there, and this was an objection I had feared all along. The moment had come to speak out.

"You should let me paint the house gray, Captain."

"What!" he exclaimed.

"The house deserves it. And the background too, with the green of the woods behind. Oh, I don't know, but the house has a style—"

"The gray style, perhaps?"

He took a few impatient strides away, then back again.

At this I became more innocent than ever: a thought came to me—it could only have come from above—and I said, '*Now* I remember! I must have seen the house manor-house gray in my mind's eye ever since—it was your wife I got it from."

I was observing him, and saw a spasm run through him. He gazed at me for a second with wide-open eyes; then he took out his handkerchief and wiped one eye as if to remove a speck of dirt.

"Really?" he said. "She said that?"

"Yes, I seem to remember it quite clearly. It was a long time ago, but—"

"It's a load of nonsense," he said, and strode away. I heard him once, over in the yard, clearing his throat noisily.

I lounged about for a while, feeling good for very little. Not daring to continue painting and thereby increase the Captain's displeasure, I spent an hour or so chopping and sawing in the woodshed. Finally I ventured back to my ladder. As I did so, the Captain stuck his head out of an upstairs window and called down, "You may just as well carry on, now that you've got so far. But I've never seen anything like it."

Then he slammed the window shut, although it had been open before.

And I painted.

A week went by; I alternated between painting and helping with the hay. Grindhusen was good enough at ridging potatoes and raking over the meadows; but his forkloads of hay were distinctly on the feeble side. As for Nils, he was a glutton for work.

One afternoon, as I was going over the house for the third time, and the elegant gray with white details was transforming the house into a residence of real style, the Captain came walking up from the road. He looked at me for a while, then took out his handkerchief as if the heat was bothering him and said, "Yes, having got so far you'd better continue. I must say, her taste wasn't bad when she said that. All the same, it's a load of nonsense. Hm!"

I made no answer.

The Captain continued, using his handkerchief the while:

"It's been hot today—pooh! What was I going to say? No, come to that, it's not bad, not bad at all. Looks as if she was right there—I mean, that's the right color you've got there. I was out in the fields just now, and I thought it looked really good. In any case, you've gone too far now."

"I agree with the Captain," I said. "It suits the house."

"Yes, it seems to suit the house. Did she say that about the woods too? My wife, I mean. Did she say that about the background?"

"It's so long ago, but I'm fairly certain—"

"Well, never mind. I must say, I'd never imagined it could be so—be just so. But aren't you going to run out of white paint?"

"Hm. No. I traded the yellow in."

At which the Captain smiled, shook his head, and walked away.

No, my instinct had not led me astray.

After that the hay took up all my time until it was finished; but in exchange Nils helped me in the evenings and spent an hour or so painting the summer-house. Even Grindhusen joined in and wielded a brush.

He was not *exactly* a painter, he said; but he figured he could be trusted to coat a wall. Grindhusen had altogether ceased being a dead weight.

And now at last the buildings all shone in their new glory, changed beyond recognition; when, for good measure, we had set to and tidied up a little in the lilac grove and the little park, Øvrebø was a different place. The Captain came and thanked each of us individually.

As we started harvesting the rye, the autumn rain started too; but we pushed ahead, cutting the rye and hanging it on stakes; and at intervals the sun came out again. There were acres of thick, fat rye, not to mention acres of barley and oats which were not yet ripe— a rich landscape to work in. The clover was starting to seed, but the turnips still had some way to go. They could do with a thorough good soaking, said Nils.

Several times the Captain employed me in fetching and carrying mail; and one day I carried a letter addressed to his wife. He handed me a bunch of letters, with the one to his wife in the middle, addressed care of her mother at Kristiansand. The first thing the Captain said when I brought back the mail that evening was, "You posted the letters all right?" I said I had.

Time passed. Then the Captain told me that, on wet days when we couldn't do much out of doors, he wanted me to do various bits of painting in the house. He showed me some enamel paints he had laid in and said, "Right: first of all, the staircase here. I want it painted white, and I've written off for a dark-red runner. Then there are various doors and windows. Only there's a certain amount of urgency over this work—I've neglected it far too long."

Beyond doubt, this was an excellent idea of the Captain's. For years he had been living it up, without a thought for how his home appeared. Now his eyes had been opened again; it was like an awakening. He showed me around, upstairs and downstairs, pointing out what needed to be done. In the course of this tour I saw pictures and busts, in the living room a big marble lion, and paintings by Askevold and Johan Christian Dahl. Heirlooms, they must have been. Madame's room upstairs still looked lived-in, with all manner of trifles laid out neatly in their places and clothes hanging on the hooks. The whole house was old and elegant, with molded ceilings, and costly wallpaper on some of the walls; but all the paintwork was yellowed or peeling. The staircase was broad and easy, with landings and a mahogany handrail.

While I was busy painting one day, the Captain came and said, "I know it's harvest time; but we need to push on with this painting too—my wife will soon be here.

I'm not sure what we'd better do. It would be nice to have it all spick-and-span."

So that letter must have been summoning Madame back! But then I reflected that it was several days since he wrote, and that since then I had been going for the post, but there had been no answer from Madame, whose writing I remembered from six years ago. The Captain doubtless imagined that he only had to say come and she would come. Well, perhaps he was right; perhaps she was just getting ready. How was I to know?

Such was the urgency over the painting that the Captain went up to the cottage in person and asked Lars to take my place and lend a hand in the fields. Not that Nils was particularly pleased by this exchange: the worthy Lars Falkenberg had little appetite for obeying orders in the place where he had once been foreman.

But the urgency over the painting proved exaggerated. The Captain sent the lad to the post a couple of times, but I watched his comings and goings, and he brought no letter from Madame. Perhaps she had not the slightest wish to come; perhaps things had reached that pass. Or she felt herself cheapened, and was too stiff and proud to answer yes when her husband called. Perhaps that was it.

But the paint was put on and had time to dry, and

the red runner was fastened with brass stair rods, and the staircase looked singularly handsome, and likewise the windows and doors in the upstairs rooms looked singularly handsome; but Madame did not come. No.

We harvested the rye, and set to work in good time cutting the barley; but Madame did not come. The Captain would stand gazing down the road, whistling; he looked thin. Time and again, when he came out to us in the fields, he would accompany us for a long time, watching us without saying a word. But if Nils asked him a question, he never needed to call back his thoughts, as it were, from a great distance, but answered at once and to the point. He was not depressed, and if he looked thin it may have been because he had got Nils to cut his hair.

But now I was sent for the post once more, and this time there was a letter from Madame. It had a Kristiansand postmark. I hurried home with the letter, put it in among the rest of the mail, and gave the bundle to the Captain, out in the courtyard. "Thanks," he said, with no apparent interest; he had grown used to being disappointed. "Everyone got their grain in? What are the roads like?" he asked, as he glanced at letter after letter. While I was answering about the state of the roads and his neighbors' grain, he reached the letter from Madame; whereupon he snapped the bundle together and started questioning me even more closely about the state of the roads and his neighbors' grain. He had schooled himself, no doubt, not to display emotion. As he went in, he thanked me again and nodded.

Next day the Captain himself set to, washing and greasing the landau. Another two days passed, however, before he needed to use it. One evening we were sitting over our supper when the Captain came into the kitchen and said he needed someone to drive him to the station in the morning. He could have driven himself, but he was fetching his wife, who had returned from a journey abroad, so he needed to take the landau in case it rained. Nils decided then and there that Grindhusen could best be spared as coachman to the Captain.

The rest of us went on with our work in the fields. There was plenty to do: apart from the rye and barley not yet under cover, there were potatoes waiting to be ridged and turnips to be weeded. At intervals, however, Ragnhild and the dairymaid gave stalwart help, setting to work like two young hurricanes.

It might have been fun to be working once again with my former mate Lars Falkenberg; but he and Nils hit it off so badly that the atmosphere in the fields was one of somber silence rather than cheerful good humor. Lars seemed to have got over some of his earlier resentment against me, but for the foreman's benefit he was short and surly with us all.

Finally Nils decided that Lars should take the pair of chestnuts and start on the autumn plowing. Lars took offense at this and flatly refused. It was the first time he had heard of anyone plowing in a field that hadn't yet been harvested! "Ah," said Nils, "but we'll find you at least a hundred acres that are harvested already."

More bickering. Everything had become so dreary and dismal at Øvrebø, Lars reckoned. In the old days he did his job and then sang songs to the master and mistress and their guests; now there was damn-all rhyme or reason in anything. "Autumn plowing, did you say? No, thank you very much!" "You don't understand these things," said Nils; "you don't realize that nowadays people plow in between the hay-drying racks or the corn poles, as the case may be." "No, I should just think I don't, said Lars, turning up the whites of his eyes; "understanding stuff like that's more in your line—you jackass, you!"

But it ended with Lars not quite daring to disobey the foreman, and agreeing to plow until the Captain returned.

It came back to me that when I went away I had left some washing with Emma. However, it seemed best to refrain from going up to the cottage to collect it, as long as Lars remained so bloody-minded.

## X

The Captain and Madame came next day. Nils and I had debated whether to hoist the flag. I couldn't quite muster the courage; but Nils had fewer qualms and went ahead. It flapped proudly and handsomely from its white mast.

I was close at hand when the master and mistress descended from the landau. Madame walked some distance into the yard, gazed at the buildings, and clapped her hands. I heard her, also, uttering loud exclamations of wonder from inside the entrance—doubtless at the sight of the staircase, with its red runner.

Grindhusen had hardly stabled the horses before coming to me all agape and taking me aside for a few words. "There must be something wrong somewhere," he began; "that can't be Mrs. Falkenberg. Is it her the Captain's married to?"

"That's correct, Grindhusen, it's his wife the Captain's married to. Why do you ask?"

"But it's the cousin! Stone me if it isn't the very same person—the Inspector of Log Driving's cousin."

"Nonsense, Grindhusen! Her sister, perhaps."

"You can stone me. I saw her any number of times with the inspector. "

"Well, all right, she could be his cousin, for that matter. What business is it of ours?"

"I saw it the moment she got off the train. And she looked at me too, and gave quite a start. She kept kind of gasping for a long while. Don't come and tell me—but what I can't make out—is she from here?"

"Did she seem happy or unhappy?"

"Can't say really—yes, I suppose so." Grindhusen shook his head, unable to grasp that this was the Captain's wife. "Surely you saw her yourself with the inspector—do you mean to say you don't recognize her?"

"Did you say she was happy?"

"Happy? Oh, I guess so. Can't say really. They talked a load of queer stuff in the carriage—no, they started talking queer at the station. There was a whole lot I couldn't make out at all. 'I'm not sure if I'm finding the right words,' she says, 'but I beg and implore you to forgive me for everything,' she says. 'And I ask the same of you,' he says. Would you believe it? And in the carriage I'll swear they were crying, both of them. 'I've had the whole place painted and done up a bit,' says the Captain. 'No, have you really?' she says. Then he talked about all her things, how they were still there and hadn't been touched; I don't know what he meant by 'things,' but that's what he said: 'I think I can safely say that they're all where you left them.' Would you believe it? 'Your things,' he said. And then he went on about someone called Elizabeth and said she was not in his thoughts and never had been—that's what it sounded like. Then the lady cried and cried and said she was sorry and carried on like she was beside herself. But she never said nothing about being abroad, like the Captain said. No, she's come from the inspector all right."

I began to fear I had been ill advised to bring Grindhusen to Øvrebø. It was done now; but I regretted my action. And I stood Grindhusen against a wall and told him so in no uncertain terms. "The mistress here has always been kindness itself to everyone, and the Captain likewise, just remember that. But you'll be out on your ass before the day's over if you go around spreading tittle-tattle. I suggest you think it over— you've got a good place here, with good wages and good food. Just remember that and keep your trap shut!"

"You're right, you know, dead right," said Grindhusen, vacillating. "I'm not denying that; I'm only saying she's the dead spit and image of that cousin. Have I ever said more than that? I don't know what's eating you. For that matter, her hair's probably a bit fairer than the cousin's was, I won't swear it's the same hair. And I never said it was. But if you want to know what I really thought from the word go, I don't mind telling you straight out that I thought she was too good to be that cousin. Those were my very thoughts. Because it was a crying shame for her to be the cousin of a fellow like that, and it beats me that anyone would want to. It's not the money I'm thinking of, mind, you know as well as I do that people like you and me don't worry about sending a two-krone piece down the drain, only it was mean giving it right into my hand and then knocking it off from my pay. Yes. I say no more. But I don't know what's been eating you lately, flying out at a man the moment he opens his mouth. What have I said, anyway? He was that tight-fisted, he only gave me two kroner a day—no board, mind—and he haggled over every blessed thing. Yes. I won't talk to you any more, but these were my very thoughts, if you really want to know…"

But for all his prattle Grindhusen was unable to gloss over the fact that he had recognized Madame and was still convinced that she was the person he thought.

And now everything was in order, the master and

mistress home again, fair days and a fat harvest. What more could we ask for?

Madame greeted me kindly and said, "Do you know, I can hardly recognize Øvrebø since you painted it so beautifully all over. The Captain's delighted with it."

She seemed calmer than when I last saw her, on the hotel stairs in the town. She didn't kind of gasp on seeing me as she had on seeing Grindhusen—and that must mean she doesn't mind seeing me again, I thought joyfully. But why had she not yet given up that new habit of flickering her eyes? If I were the Captain, I would speak to her about it. In addition, a number of curious little pimples had appeared about her temples, though these made no difference to her looks.

"But I'm sorry to say it wasn't my idea, this beautiful gray for the walls," she continued. "Your memory's at fault there."

"Well, I can't make it out. But it makes no difference in any case—it was the Captain himself who decided on it."

"The staircase is quite exquisite; so are the rooms upstairs. They're twice as cheerful now…"

It was Madame herself who wished to be twice as cheerful and twice as good—that much was clear to me. For some reason or other, she felt she owed me these courtesies, and I thought: Good—but now that is enough, let it rest there!

Autumn was setting in: the scent from the jasmine in the grove was strong and importunate, while up on the wooded slopes the leaves had long since turned yellow and red. There was not a soul in the place but rejoiced at Madame's return. The flag, too, helped make it seem like a Sunday, with the girls in newly ironed aprons.

In the evening I went down the stone steps into the grove and sat there. After the heat of the day, waves of scent from the jasmine were wafted toward me. Then Nils came down, looking for me. He said, "No more guests here now—and no more racketing around either, that I've heard. Have you heard any racketing around at night since the Captain came back from maneuvers?"

"No."

"And that was a good ten weeks ago. What do you say to my cutting this off right now?" Nils asked, indicating his temperance badge. "The Captain's left off drinking, Madame's home again, and there's no need for me to go around being mean to either of them."

Whereupon he handed me his knife and I cut the badge away.

We talked for a while about the fields—he had fields

on the brain. "Yes," he said, "by tomorrow evening, thank God, we'll have most of the grain in. After that we'll sow the winter rye. Isn't it strange, here's Lars been using the machine to sow with, year after year, and thinking that was good enough. No, no; we're going to sow by hand."

"But why?"

"On land like ours! You take a look at the next property over that way: he sowed by machine three weeks ago—some of it's come up, some of it hasn't. The machine loosens the soil too much."

"Mmm—just smell the jasmine this evening!"

"Yes. The barley and oats have come on a lot these last few days. Well, I guess it's time to go to bed."

Nils got up, but I remained seated. Nils surveyed the sky and prophesied a fine morning; then he talked a little about cutting some of the excellent second crop of hay which the meadow here had produced.

"Are you going on sitting there?" he asked suddenly.

"Yes, why? No, perhaps I'd better be going too."

Nils took a few steps, then returned and said, "You shouldn't sit here any longer. You ought to come with me."

"Should I?" I said, and rose at once; I realized that Nils had come here on purpose to fetch me, for some reason of his own.

Could he have seen through me? But what was there to see through? Did even I know what I had gone to the grove for? I remember lying there on my stomach, chewing a straw. There was a light in a certain upstairs room in the main building; and this I was looking at. That was all.

"I don't want to be inquisitive, but what's up?" I asked.

"Nothing," Nils answered. "The girls said you were lying here, and so I came down. Why should anything be up?"

So the girls must have seen through me, I thought dejectedly. That'll be Ragnhild, the confounded girl—and she's so sharp, she's certainly said much more than Nils here wants to come out with. And what if Madame herself has seen me from her window?

I resolved to be indifferent and cold as ice for the rest of my days.

Ragnhild was in her element: the thick stair carpet muffled her footsteps—she could go up whenever she wanted and down again in a flash without a sound, if the need arose.

"I can't make Madame out," said Ragnhild. "Now she's come back, she ought to be happy and nice, but all she does is whine and cry. The Captain said to her today, 'Do be a bit reasonable, Louise,' he said. 'I'm sorry, I won't do it any more,' she said, and cried because she'd been unreasonable. But that bit about not doing it any more—she's said that every day now since she came home, and still she goes on doing it. Poor thing, she had such a bad toothache today, she was howling—"

"Look, go and lift some more potatoes, Ragnhild!" Nils broke in. "We haven't time to stand around talking today."

And so back to the fields again for one and all. Oh, how much there was to do! Nils was afraid of the corn spoiling on the poles, and preferred getting it in on the damp side. Fair enough. But that meant threshing the worst of it at once, and spreading the grain over every outbuilding floor in the place; even the floor of the great servants' hall had a layer of corn lying there to dry. Any more irons in the fire? Yes, any number more, and all white hot. The weather had turned nasty and might get worse, and none of the work would brook delay. After threshing we had the fresh straw to cut up and salt down in bins, or it might spoil. That the lot? Far from it, many irons still glowing. Grindhusen and the girls were taking up potatoes. Nils was using the precious time after a couple of dry days to sow some three acres of rye, while the lad did a good job harrowing in his wake; and Lars Falkenberg was still plowing. The good Lars had knuckled under and become a mighty plowman since the Captain's return with Madame; when the cornfields were too wet, he plowed the meadows; then, after a few days' sun and wind, he plowed in the cornfields again.

All went smoothly and well. One afternoon the Captain himself came out in the field and lent a hand. We were bringing in the last of the corn.

Captain Falkenberg was no mean worker: big and strong, with a capable pair of hands. He was loading up oats from the drying frames, and was on his second load.

At this point Madame came walking along the road; then she cut across to the drying frames, where we were working. Her eyes were bright, and she seemed to enjoy the sight of her husband loading up corn.

"Bless the work!" she said.

"Thank you," said her husband.

"We used to say that up north," she continued.

"What?"

"We used to say that up north."

"I see."

The Captain went on working, and the crackling of the stubble meant that he did not always hear what she said and had to ask her to repeat herself. This irritated them both.

"Are the oats ripe?" she asked.

"Yes, thank God."

"But they're not dry, are they?"

"I can't hear you!"

"Oh, nothing."

A long, sullen silence. From time to time the Captain tried to put in a cheerful word, but met with no response.

"So you're making a tour of inspection, eh?" he said, attempting humor. "Have you been over to the potato field?"

"No. But I'll gladly go there if you can't bear the sight of me here."

It was so unpleasant that I may well have expressed distaste with my eyebrows. Moreover, I suddenly remembered that I had a particular reason for being as cold as ice, and this made me wrinkle my brows still more.

Madame looked straight at me and said, "Why are you pulling a face?"

"What—pulling faces, are you?" said the Captain, with a forced laugh.

Madame rounded on him. "You heard *that* all right!"

"Come, come, Louise," said the Captain.

The tears welled up into her eyes. For a moment she stood there; then, leaning forward from the waist, she ran behind the drying frames and burst into sobs.

The Captain followed her.

"What is it, Louise, can you tell me?"

"Oh, it's nothing. Do go away!"

I could hear her vomiting now behind the frames, and wailing, "Oh, God help me!"

"My wife isn't at all well at present," the Captain remarked to me. "We're all puzzled by what it is."

"There's supposed to be a bug going around," I said, by way of saying something. "A kind of autumn flu; I heard it at the post office."

"Really? Do you hear that, Louise?" he called. "There's a bug going around—it must be that you've got."

Madame didn't answer.

We continued loading up from the frames, while Madame moved farther and farther along as we approached her. Finally she lost her last shred of cover and stood there as if caught in some act. She was very pale after her nausea.

"Shall I see you home?" asked the Captain.

"No, thanks. Quite unnecessary," she answered, starting to go.

And the Captain stayed with us until evening, loading up the corn.

But now everything was in chaos again. How difficult life was for the Captain and his wife!

And, of course, it was not a thing that could be put right with a little goodwill on each side, as sensible people say; it was something insurmountable, a disharmony at the deepest level of their beings. It had culminated with one of the marriage partners in a state of mutiny: Madame now locked her door at night. Ragnhild had heard the Captain speaking in injured tones through the wall.

But that evening the Captain had demanded and obtained an audience with his wife in her room, before she went to bed, and there had been a new fracas. Each, no doubt, desperately wanted to put things right. But this was beyond their powers; they had left it till too late. Nils and I sat in the kitchen listening to Ragnhild; I had never seen Nils so despondent.

"If things go wrong again now," he said, "it's the end. I kept wondering, in the summer, if perhaps what she needed was a good thrashing; now I can see that would have been madness. Did she say she was leaving him again?"

"She hinted as much," said Ragnhild, and proceeded to tell her story, somewhat as follows: "It started with the Captain asking if she didn't think it was this stomach bug she'd got. But she said it was hardly a stomach bug, her taking such a dislike to him. 'Have you really taken such a dislike to me?' 'Yes, I could scream. That awful habit you have of eating vast quantities of food.' 'Do I?' says the Captain. 'I don't know if that's an awful habit exactly, it's the way I'm made—there are no fixed rules about the size of meals.' 'Yes, but watching you all the time makes me throw up—that's the reason I keep throwing up.' 'Well,' he says, 'at least I don't drink too much any more—so surely things are a bit better than they were.' 'On the contrary, they're much worse.' Then the Captain says, 'To be quite frank, I think you might try and be a bit patient with me after I've—after what you did in the summer.' 'Yes, you're right,' says Madame, and then she starts crying. 'It gnaws and gnaws at me night and day,' he says, 'but I've never once mentioned it.' 'No, I know,' she says, and cries more than ever.

"'And what's more,' he says, 'it was I who asked you to come back.' But then she must have thought he was totting up the score too much, because she stops crying and tosses her head and says, 'Yes, and you'd have done far better not to have written to me if this was all you were bringing me back to.' 'And what may that be?' he asks; 'you do just as you please, and always have; only you take no interest in anything—you don't even touch your piano; all you do is go around being touchy and difficult and thinking nothing's good enough for you. And then you shut your door on me at night. That's fine by me, just carry on shutting it!' And she answers, 'You're the one who's touchy and difficult, if you ask me. I never go to bed at night or get up in the morning without being in terror of my life in case you should be reminded of that business in the summer. Never once mentioned it, did you say? Oh no, indeed. Oh *yes*, my friend, you never go five minutes without rubbing my nose in it. There was one day when I made a slip of the tongue and said Hugo—and what did you do? You could easily have patted my hand gently and helped me over it, but all you did was sneer and say, "I'm not Hugo, you know." Well, of course I knew you weren't Hugo, and I was really and truly sorry about what I'd said.'

" 'That's precisely the point,' says the Captain; 'are you really and truly sorry about that Hugo business?' 'Yes,' says Madame, 'I'm really and truly sorry about it.' 'I don't believe you are—seems to me you're as standoffish as ever.' 'And what about you then? Haven't you by any chance got something to be sorry about?' 'Haven't you got photographs of Hugo standing on your piano to this very day? And have you ever shown any sign of removing them, even though I've made it clear, not once but fifty times, how much I wanted it—positively begged you to do so?' 'How you do harp on those photographs!' she says. 'Look, don't get me wrong: if you go and remove them now, it no longer means a thing to me, after I've coaxed you about it fifty times or more. Only it would have been a little less shameless if of your own free will you'd burned those pictures the day you came home. Instead of which, you've still got books with his name in floating about in your room. And there's a handkerchief with his initials on, I see.' 'Sheer jealousy on your part,' says Madame; 'why should a thing like that matter? I can't kill him, much as you'd like it, and Mama and Papa say the same. After all, I've lived with him and been married to him.' 'Married to him?' 'That's what I said. It's not everyone who looks at Hugo and me as you do.' After that the Captain sat there for a long time shaking his head. 'And in any case, it's all your own fault,' says Madame after a while; 'driving off with Elizabeth that time, even after I'd come and begged you to stay at home. That was when it happened. And we'd had a lot to drink that evening, my head was going round and round.' The Captain still sits there saying nothing; then he says, 'Yes, it was wrong of me to go away that time.'

'Yes, it was,' says Madame, and starts crying again. 'You wouldn't listen to anything. And you're always rubbing my nose in it over Hugo, and forgetting what you yourself have done.' 'There's only one small difference,' says the Captain; 'namely, that I've never lived with the lady you have in mind, never been married to her, as you call it.' Madame just cocks an eyebrow at that. 'Never!' says the Captain, and hits the table with his fist. Madame jumps a foot, then sits there staring at him. 'Then perhaps,' she says, 'you can explain why you were always running after her and sitting in the summerhouse with her and lurking in all the dark corners?' 'It was you who sat in the summerhouse,' he says. Then she says, 'That's right, it's always me, never you!' 'No,' says the Captain, 'the reason why I ran after Elizabeth was simply to get you back. You'd drifted away from me and I wanted you back again.' Madame sits and thinks about that for a moment; then she jumps up and throws her arms around him and says, 'Then you loved me after all! And I thought it was all over. Because you'd been drifting away from me too, for years—you remember? What a mess it all was! I never thought—I never knew—and to think it was me you loved all the time! But goodness me, then everything's all right again!'

"'Sit down,' he says. 'There's only this to remember, of course that something has happened since then.' 'Happened? What?' 'You see, you've forgotten already. May I ask now if you're at all sorry about what's happened?' Then Madame gets all wound up again and says, 'Oh, you mean Hugo. That's over and done with now.' 'You haven't answered my question.' 'Whether I'm really and truly sorry about it? And you—are you so utterly blameless?' Then the Captain gets up and starts pacing up and down. 'Our trouble is not having any children,' says Madame. 'I've no daughter I can bring up to be better than I am.' 'I've thought about that,' says the Captain, 'and perhaps you're right.' And then he turns and looks straight at her and says, 'It's as if a vicious landslide has swept over us, Louise. But we've survived—shouldn't we set to work now and clear away all the stones and tree trunks and gravel that have been burying us for years and start breathing again? You could still have a daughter!' Then Madame gets up and wants to say something, only she can't get it out. All she can say is 'Yes' and then 'Yes' again. 'You're tired now and your nerves are on edge, but think about it later. Good night, Louise.' And 'Good night,' says Madame."

## XI

The Captain told Nils that he had it in mind to put all his logging out on contract, or alternatively, to sell the standing timber. Nils took this to mean that he wished to avoid taking on more new people. "It looks as if he and his wife are back to square one."

Once we had lifted the potatoes, the immediate pressure was removed. But we still had plenty to do: the autumn plowing was behind schedule, and Lars Falkenberg and I were both kept busy on this now—fields and meadows alike.

That singular creature, Nils, now found Øvrebø so depressing again that he would gladly have given notice and gone, but the shame of abandoning his service was more than he could endure. He had strong, clear views about honor, views handed down through many generations: a boy from a large farm did not behave like a boy from a small holding. Besides, he had not been there long enough yet: before he came, Øvrebø had been shamefully neglected, and it would take many years to get the place back on its feet. This year, with the extra help he had had, was the first in which he had managed to gain some ground. But from now onward he could start seeing the fruits of his toil—look at the harvest this year, look at that fine heavy grain! And the

Captain had had occasion, for the first time in many years, to look at this rich harvest with wonder and gratitude. He could sell by the bushel.

But in that case it made no sense for Nils to leave Øvrebø. He needed, however, to pay a flying visit to his home, a bit to the north; and to this end he took two days' leave when all the potatoes were harvested. We speculated on his purpose, which must surely be a valid one—perhaps to see his girl. He returned the same straightforward, active fellow as ever and resumed his work.

As we sat in the kitchen one lunchtime, we saw Madame come rushing out of the house and away down the drive in the greatest agitation. The Captain followed, calling, "Louise—no, *Louise*—where are you going?" But Madame's only answer was "Leave me alone!"

We all looked at each other, and Ragnhild left the table to follow Madame.

"That's right," said Nils, calmly as always. "Only first go in the living room and see if she's removed those photographs."

"They're still there," answered Ragnhild as she left the room.

Out in the yard, we heard the Captain say, "Go and look for the mistress, Ragnhild."

No one thought of leaving Madame to her fate; everyone felt concerned about her.

On our way back to the fields, Nils said to me, "She ought to remove those photographs. It's not right of her to leave them there. She's a changed person."

I thought: What do you know about it? I, of course, was full of wisdom about people, after all I had learned on my wanderings. Perhaps our foreman was merely taking up a stance. I decided to test him a little.

"I find it strange," I said, "that the Captain hasn't taken those pictures and burned them long ago."

"I don't," Nils answered. "I wouldn't have done so either."

"Really?"

"It would be for her to do it, not for me."

We walked on a little. Then Nils said something that showed the soundness and depth of his instinct. "Poor Madame! I don't think she's ever got over that false step of hers in the summer; it's done her an injury. That's how I see it: there are some who pick themselves up after a fall and continue on their way through life, with their blue and yellow bruises. And there are others who never rise again."

"Well," I said, still testing him, "she certainly has the appearance of taking it lightly enough."

"One can't tell," he answered; "but to my mind she's

been a changed person ever since. She has to live, of course; but perhaps her harmony is gone. I'm no judge in these matters, but it's harmony I mean. No, of course she can eat and laugh and sleep, but…I've just seen someone like that into the grave."

At this I stopped being wise and unbending, and was foolish and ashamed. I could only say, "You have? She died?"

"Yes. That's what she wanted most." Suddenly he said, "Right, carry on plowing, you and Lars. We haven't got all that much left."

And with that he went his way and I went mine.

I thought perhaps it was a sister of his that had got into trouble, that he'd just been seeing into her grave. Dear God, there are indeed some who never get over it; it shakes them to their foundations, like a revolution. It all depends on how coarse-fibered they are! Blue and yellow bruises, Nils said…A thought struck me and I stopped dead: perhaps it was not his sister but his girl!

Some association of ideas made me think of my washing. I decided to send the lad up to the cottage for it.


Evening.

Ragnhild came to my room and begged me to stay awake again—everything was at sixes and sevens with the master and mistress. She was greatly agitated, and now in the dusk the only place she dared to sit was on my knee. It was always the same: under the stress of emotion she grew timid and tender, timid and tender.

"Can you leave the kitchen like this?" I asked. "Is anyone taking your place?"

"Yes, the cook's listening for the bell. Do you know," she announced, "I'm on the Captain's side—I've been on his side all along."

"That's only because he's a man."

"No, it's not."

"And you ought to be on the mistress's side."

"You only say that because she's a woman," Ragnhild retorted. "But you don't know all that I know. Madame's so unreasonable. Saying we don't care about her, saying we just let her go to rack and ruin. Did you ever hear the like—when I'd run after her and all? And the dreadful way she's behaved!"

"I don't want to hear about it," I said.

"But I haven't been listening—are you crazy? I was there in the same room and heard them."

"I see. In that case, we'll stay here till you've calmed down a little; then we'll go down and join Nils."

And so timid and tender was Ragnhild that she threw her arms around me for being kind. She really was an extraordinary girl.

And so we went down and joined Nils. I said,

"Ragnhild thinks one of us ought to stay awake a bit longer."

"It's so sad down there, you see," said Ragnhild; "worse than it's ever been. God knows what the Captain's going to do—maybe he won't even go to bed. Oh, she loves the Captain all right, and the Captain loves her too; only everything's gone wrong. When she ran off today, the Captain was in the yard and said to me, 'Go and find the mistress, Ragnhild!' So I went and found her—there she was, standing behind a tree by the side of the road, just standing there crying and smiling at me. I wanted her to come in again, but she said we didn't care about her—it made no difference where she went. 'The Captain's sent me to find Madame,' I said. 'Has he?' she asked. 'Now? Has he sent you just now?' 'Yes,' I said. 'Wait a bit then!' she said. She stood there for quite a while; then she said, 'Will you take those detestable books lying in my room and burn them? No, I'll do it myself,' she said, 'but I'll ring for you after supper, and then you must come up straightaway.' 'Very good,' I said. And then I got her to come with me.

"And to think she's with child," said Ragnhild suddenly. We looked at each other. The foreman's face became indistinct and blurred; he shriveled up, his eyes seemed to go to sleep. Why did he take it so much to heart?

To break the silence, I said, "Madame was going to ring, did she say?"

"Yes, and she rang. There was something she wanted to say to the Captain, but she was scared and wanted to have me with her. 'Light a candle,' she says to me, 'and then pick up all these hundred and one buttons that I've dropped.' Then she calls to the Captain in his room. So I light a candle and start picking up buttons, dozens and dozens of them, all sorts and sizes. The Captain comes, and Madame immediately says to him, 'I only wanted to say how kind you were, sending Ragnhild to look for me today. God bless you for it!' 'Well, well,' he says, smiling, 'you *were* a bundle of nerves, my dear.' 'It's true,' she says, 'my nerves are bad, but I hope it'll get better. The trouble is my not having a daughter that I could bring up to be a really nice girl. There's nothing left for me to do.' The Captain sits down on a chair. 'Surely there is,' he says. 'Surely there is, did you say? Oh, I know it says in that book over there—ugh, those wretched books—take them away and burn them, Ragnhild!' she says; then she says, 'No, I'm going to tear them to shreds myself and throw them in that stove.' And she starts pulling the books to pieces, taking a handful of pages at a time and throwing them in the stove. 'Don't let your nerves run away with you so, Louise!' says the Captain. *'The Monastery,'* she says—that's the book in her hand. 'But I can't go into a monastery, or even a convent. So there's nothing left for me to do. When I laugh, you think I'm laughing,' she says to the Captain; 'but really I'm taking it seriously and not laughing at all.' 'Is your toothache better?' he asks. 'You know very well my toothache won't be better for a long time yet.' 'I know nothing of the kind.' 'Don't you?' 'No.' 'Good God, can't you *see* what's the matter with me?' she says. The Captain just looks at her and doesn't say anything. 'Why, I'm—oh, you said today I could still have a daughter, don't you remember?' I happened to look up at the Captain…"

Ragnhild smiled and shook her head. Then she continued, "God forgive me for laughing, but the Captain's face was so funny—he looked like a half-wit. 'Haven't you realized that before now?' says Madame. The Captain looks my way and says, 'What's that you're doing all this time?' 'I asked her to pick up all my buttons for me,' says Madame. 'I've finished now,' I said. 'Have you?' says Madame, getting up; 'let me see.' And she takes the box and drops the buttons all over the floor again—rolled everywhere, they did, under the table and the bed and the stove everywhere. 'Did you ever see such a mess?' says Madame. But then off she goes again on her own tack. 'Well, fancy your not realizing that I—what was wrong with me.' 'Can't those buttons stay there till the morning?' says the Captain. 'Yes, I suppose so,' says Madame, 'except that I'll be treading all over them. I'm not good at—I'm hardly capable of picking up but never mind, let them lie there,' she says, and starts stroking his hand. 'Darling, darling!' she says. But then he takes his hand away. 'Ah, now you're angry with me,' she says; 'but then why did you write to me?' 'My dear Louise, we're not alone,' he says. 'Surely you must know why you wrote to me?' 'I suppose I hoped things would turn out all right.' 'But they didn't?' 'Well, no.' 'But what was in your mind when you sat down and wrote to me? Me? You wanted me again? I can't make out what was in your mind.' 'Ah, Ragnhild's finished, I see,' says the Captain. 'Good night, Ragnhild!'"

"So off you went?"

"Yes, but I didn't dare go very far from Madame. You can imagine the pickle she was in when I went—I had to be somewhere handy. And if the Captain had come and said anything, I'd have told him straight that I had no intention of going any farther off, with Madame in the state she was. Not that he came, as it happened; they only started talking again in there. 'I know what you're going to say,' says Madame; 'it could be that it's not you who—it could be that you're not the father. Yes, I think perhaps you may be, after all. Only I wish to God I could find words to make you forgive me,' she says, sobbing. 'Say you do, dearest, say you do!' she sobs; and then she goes down on her knees on the floor. 'You've seen me now getting rid of the books, and that handkerchief with the initials on I've burned already, and look, there are the books—' 'Yes, and there's another handkerchief with the same initials,' says the Captain; 'goodness, how considerate you are toward me, Louise!' Madame gets all upset. 'I'm sorry you should have seen that,' she says; 'it must have come back with me in the summer, and I keep forgetting to go through my things. But does it really matter so very much? Well?' 'Of course not,' he says. 'And if you'd only listen to me for a moment,' she says, 'it's very likely you who—I mean, that it's your child. Why shouldn't it be? It's just that I don't know how to put it.' 'Do get up off your knees,' says the Captain. But Madame must have misunderstood him, because she stands up and says, 'There you are—you won't listen to me. But in that case I'm jolly well going to ask you why you wrote to me at all, instead of leaving me alone.' The Captain says something about a man who's grown up in a prison yard—that was what he called it. Take him out of his prison yard, he said, and he'll long for it again—something like that. 'Yes,' she says, 'but I stayed with Papa and Mama, and they weren't as hard as you are—they said I'd been married to him, and they weren't at all unreasonable with me. Not everyone looks at it as you do.' 'Why don't you blow out that candle that Ragnhild was using?' says the Captain. 'It looks silly standing next to the lamp—almost as if it was ashamed.' 'Ashamed of me, I suppose,' she says; 'yes, that's what you meant. But you've been greatly to blame as well.' 'Don't misunderstand me,' he says quickly; 'I know I've been greatly to blame—but nothing for you to make a song and dance about.' 'That's what you think. Well, of all the—so you're blameless, are you?' 'I didn't say that. For many years I've been to blame—does that satisfy you? But not in the way you mean. And I certainly don't come home to you carrying the fruits of my blameworthiness under my heart.' 'No,' says Madame, 'but you were really the one who never wanted me to get—never wanted us to have children; and if I didn't either, it was up to you to know better. That's what they said at home, too. Because if I'd had a daughter—' 'You can spare us that magazine story,' says the Captain. 'But it's true,' says Madame; 'how can you possibly deny it?' 'I'm not denying anything. Do sit still and listen to me, Louise. These children and this daughter you keep plugging away at are something you've picked up quite recently. And the moment you came across the idea you made it your hope and salvation. But you never made children an issue before that I ever heard.' 'Yes, but you ought to have known better.' 'That's something else you've picked up recently. Still, this is beside the point—it may well be that we'd have done better to have had children. I've come to realize that for myself—too late, unfortunately. And look at the state of you now!' 'Oh God, yes! But perhaps you *are*—I don't know—no, I suppose not…' 'Me?' says the Captain, and shakes his head. 'Oh, it *ought* to be the mother who knows, of course; but in this instance it seems she doesn't. In this marriage of mine the mother doesn't know. Or do you?' Madame says nothing to that. 'Do you know? I'm asking you.' Still she says nothing—just collapses on the floor and cries. Honestly, I don't know—perhaps I'm on Madame's side after all—it was *dreadful* for her. In the end I was going to knock and go in, but then the Captain started off again. 'You don't say anything,' he says. 'But that too is an answer. It's as clear as if you'd shouted it from the rooftops.' 'I can't say more,' says Madame, and cries and cries. 'There're many things I love you for, Louise,' says the Captain, 'and one of them's your truthfulness.' 'Thank you,' she says. 'They haven't yet taught you to lie. Get up, now.' And he helps her up and settles her on her chair again—it was pitiful to see how she cried. 'Be quiet, now,' he says. 'I want to ask you something: shall we wait and see what it looks like, what sort of eyes it has, and so on?' 'Yes, God bless you—let's do that! Oh darling, darling, God bless you!' 'And I shall simply try to bear it. It gnaws and gnaws at me, but…And I too am to blame.' 'God bless you! God bless you!' she says again. 'And you too!' he says. 'Good night now—see you in the morning.' Then Madame flops forward over the table and cries as if her heart's going to break. 'What are you crying about now?' he asks. 'Because you're going,' she says; 'earlier on, I was afraid of you—now I'm crying because you're going. Couldn't you stay a little?' 'Here? With you, now?' he asks. 'No, I didn't mean—it wasn't that,' she says; 'but I'm so lonely. Oh no, I didn't mean what you think.' 'Ah well, I'm going now,' says the Captain; 'you must surely understand that I don't particularly feel like staying here any longer. Ring for the maid.'

"So off I ran," Ragnhild concluded.

After a while Nils asked, "Have they gone to bed now?"

Ragnhild didn't know. Yes, perhaps; but in any case the cook was keeping an eye on things. "But good heavens, what a mess Madame's got herself into—I can't imagine her being able to sleep."

"You'd better pop over and see how she is."

"Yes," said Ragnhild, getting up. "No, honestly, I'm more on the Captain's side, whatever you may say. Yes, really and truly. "

"It's not so easy to know what's right."

"Just imagine being got with child by *him*! How could she do such a thing? And she's been staying with him in that town since then, or so I hear—what sense is there in that? And all those handkerchiefs of his I've seen, and any number of hers missing—they must have been using each other's. Lived with him, she said! When she had a husband and all!"


## XII


The Captain had done what he'd said and had put the logging out on contract: there came a cracking and a crashing from the forest. It was a mild autumn, too, with no frost as yet—good plowing weather. Nils piled up the hours like a miser, to lighten the burden of work in the spring.

The question arose whether Grindhusen and I

should join in the logging. I remembered that really I ought now to be on my way to the region where the berries grow, to the mountains thick with cloudberries—what about that journey? As for Grindhusen, he was hardly much use to the Captain as a logger nowadays: all he was fit for was to hang around and hold one end of a saw from time to time.

No, Grindhusen had grown sluggish—devil only knows how to explain it. He still had all his hair, and that hair was still red. But he had picked up nicely at Øvrebø, thank you, and maintained the appetite and digestion of an ox. How he flourished! All that summer and autumn he had sent regular sums of money home to his family; and he poured out his panegyrics about the Captain and his wife, who paid so reasonably and were such a model master and mistress. Not like the inspector, who haggled and dickered over every little dre and ended up, so help me God, knocking off two kroner, which he'd fairly and squarely—ah shit! He, Grindhusen, would cheerfully send a two-krone piece down the drain if it served any earthly use or purpose; but bloody hell! Catch the Captain doing a thing like that !

But Grindhusen was so evasive and vacillating nowadays; he couldn't even get properly angry with anyone. He might yet go back to the Inspector of Log Driving for two kroner a day, and say a faithful yea to his every word. Age and time had caught up with him.

As they catch up with us all.

The Captain said, "That water pipe you mentioned once—is it too late in the year to do anything about it now?"

"Yes," I said.

The Captain nodded and walked away.

I did another day's plowing; then the Captain came to me again. He was here, there, and everywhere these days, working hard himself and keeping an eye on everything. He barely finished his food before he was out again: in barn and stable, in the fields, in the forest with the loggers.

"You may as well get cracking on that water pipe," he said. "It could be quite a while yet before the first frost. Who do you want helping you?"

"Grindhusen can help me," I answered. "But—"

"Right, and Lars. What were you going to say?"

"We *could* start getting frosts any day now."

"Or we could get snow, in which case there'd be no hard frosts. We don't get hard frosts every winter here, not by any means. You'd better take several men with you, and have some of them digging, others doing masonry work. I take it you've done this kind of work before?"

"Yes."

"I've warned Nils, so you don't need to be afraid of any unpleasantness," he said with a smile. "Now take the horses in."

He was so impatient that I too caught the itch to plunge right in, and ran rather than walked the horses home. The Captain had set his heart on this water supply after seeing the beauty of the newly painted house and the richness of the harvest. And now he was cutting his thousand dozen battens, and paying off his debt, with something to spare!

So I set off uphill and rediscovered the site that I had long since earmarked for the reservoir; then I took a bearing on the house below me, paced out the distance, measured and calculated. There was a stream with its source far up the hill; its channel was so deep, and its fall such, that it never froze in winter. At the chosen spot I intended to build a small reservoir, with built-in overflow outlets for the spring and autumn flood waters. Yes, Øvrebø would get its water supply all right. Our building materials we would quarry in sits—there was layer upon layer of granite.

By noon next day the work was in full swing: Lars Falkenberg was digging the trench for the pipeline, Grindhusen and I quarrying—work we both knew well from our road-building days at Skreia.

Good.

We worked for four days; then it was Sunday. I remember that Sunday: high, clear sky, the trees stripped of their leaves, the hills green and peaceful on every side, smoke from the cottage chimney rising into the air. In the afternoon Lars Falkenberg had borrowed a horse and cart from the Captain to drive his newly slaughtered pig to the station en route for the town. On his way home Lars was to collect the Captain's mail.

It occurred to me that this was a suitable evening for sending the lad to fetch my washing from the cottage: Lars was away, and no one need be offended by that washing any more.

Oh yes, I said to myself, your motives are impeccable, sending the lad for the washing. Only it's not a case of having worthy motives, or any motives at all; mark my words, it's merely old age.

I chewed on this for an hour or so. Yes: most probably I'd been deluding myself with a lot of nonsense. Besides, it was a singularly mild evening, Sunday at that, nothing to do, the servants' hall deserted. Decrepitude of old age? Hills getting too much for me?

So I made the journey.

Early next morning Lars Falkenberg was down at the manor again. He took me aside, as once before, and for the self-same purpose. I had been up at the cottage yesterday; it was for the last time—just remember that!

"It was also the last piece of washing," I pointed out.

"Washing, washing, washing! Couldn't I have brought you that miserable shirt of yours a hundred times this autumn?"

"I didn't want to remind you of that washing again."

What witchcraft was this, that he had already heard about my little walk yesterday evening? The insufferable Ragnhild must have been out telling tales; there was no one else it could have been.

As fate would have it, Nils, our foreman, was close at hand on this occasion too. He came innocently across the yard from the kitchen—and at once replaced me as the main target for Lars's rancor.

"Ah, here comes the other caricature too," said Lars. "And he looks even more of an insult to his Creator."

"What's that you're saying?" asked Nils.

"What's that you're saying?" retorted Lars. "Go and rinse your mouth out with some patent mouthwash or other, and speak intelligibly."

Nils stopped to see what it was all about, and said, "I don't understand a word of all this."

"You don't, huh? Understand, huh? No, indeed! Plowing in uncut corn, that's what you understand. When it comes to understanding that, there's no one to touch you."

Nils's cheeks turned pale with unaccustomed anger,

and he said, "You really are an incorrigible fool, Lars! Can't you shut your trap and stop talking baloney for once?"

"Fool, eh? Just listen to that jackass," said Lars, turning to me. "Doesn't he talk posh? 'Incorrigible,' he says—and turns pale with the effort...I've spent more years than you at Øvrebø, *and* I've sung to the master and mistress more than once of an evening, let me tell you. Whereas nowadays it's nothing but maundering and megalomania. You remember"—turning to me again—"what it was like here in the old days? It was Lars here and Lars there, and I never heard of the work not getting done. And after me came Albert—he was in charge for eighteen months. And after Albert came you, Nils. And now it's all pushing people around and plowing and carting manure day and night, so to speak, till a man goes as thin as a frostbitten fingertip with it all."

At this point Nils and I were unable to keep a straight face. Far from being offended, Lars felt he had made a hit as a humorist; he was instantly appeased and joined in the laughter himself.

"Yes, I'm telling you straight," he said. "And if it wasn't for the fact that at times you're quite a nice lad—nice? No, I won't go as far as that, but helpful and pleasant in a way—if it wasn't for that, then—"

"Yes, what would happen then?"

Lars had become more and more good-humored; he laughed and answered, "Well, I suppose I could always pick you up and stuff you into your own boots."

"Want to feel my arm?" said Nils.

"What's going on?" asked the Captain, walking toward us. It was only six o'clock, but he was already up and about.

"Nothing," said Lars; and "Nothing," said Nils.

"How's the reservoir going?" the Captain asked me. But without waiting for an answer, he turned to Nils and said, "I need the boy now to drive me to the station. I'm off to Christiania."

Grindhusen and I resumed our work on the reservoir, and Lars his digging. But a cloud had come over our spirits.

"Pity about the Captain going away," even Grindhusen acknowledged.

I felt the same. But of course the Captain had business to transact—timber and crops to sell. Only why was he leaving so early in the day? He couldn't, in any case, catch the morning train. Had there been conflict again? Did he wish to be gone before his wife was up?

And indeed there was often conflict.

It had now reached the point where the Captain and

Madame no longer made any perceptible movement of the lips when they spoke to each other; if obliged to exchange a few words, they did so in tones of complete indifference, their eyes well and truly averted. From time to time the Captain might look his wife in the face and urge her to go out and enjoy the fine weather; once he even called to her to come in from the courtyard and play a little on her piano. But this, I suspect, was done for the sake of appearances, and for no other reason.

How sad it all was!

Madame was quiet and pretty; sometimes she would stand outside on the steps, with her soft features and reddish-yellow hair, gazing up at the hills. Already she looked like a good young mother. But the place was utterly desolate for her now—no visitors any more, no games or music, no joy; only sorrow and shame.

The Captain had, of course, promised to bear his burden for the present; and doubtless he bore what he could. More he could not do. A calamity had struck the house; and a calamity is harder to bear than seven burdens. If Madame in a hasty moment forgot to show gratitude, the Captain would look down at the floor and shortly afterward take his hat and go out. The maids could all quote instances of this, and I myself witnessed it once or twice. Naturally, he could never forget her faux pas—no, never. Still, he could keep quiet about it. But how was he to keep quiet about it when she forgot herself and said, "You *know* I'm not well, you *know* I can't walk as much as usual"? He would frown and answer, "Hush, Louise!" And the conflict would be in full swing: "Do you have to keep reminding me of it?" "On the contrary, it's you yourself who keeps reminding us both of it; you've lost your modesty since your fall, you've become brazen and shameless." "Oh, why did I come back here? I was far better off at home." "Yes, or with the whelp." "I thought you said he helped you once? Yes, dear God, I often wish I was back with Hugo—he's worth any number of you."

Her words were completely irresponsible; possibly they went further than she herself intended. But she had become unrecognizable to us all—and corrupt. Mrs. Falkenberg corrupt? Perhaps not—God alone knows. Be that as it may, she had the nerve to come out into the kitchen of an evening and address flattering words to Nils about his youth and strength. I suppose I was a little jealous again, and envied the foreman his youth, for I thought: Has everyone gone mad? Surely we older men are much to be preferred! Was it Nils's innocence that had caught her eye? Or was she merely keeping her end up, trying to be younger than she was? But then one day she came up to the reservoir and sat for a while watching Grindhusen and me. For half an hour the work was child's play, the granite amenable and obedient to our wills, and we ourselves a Herculean pair of stonemasons. Yes, but she was being irresponsible again, playing around with her eyes. Why did she not cure herself of this new habit? Her eyes were too grave for such a game; it didn't suit her. I thought: Either she's using Grindhusen and me to cancel out her foolishness with Nils, or she's playing a new game, for new stakes. But which? I couldn't make up my mind. As for Grindhusen, he understood nothing—all he said when Madame went away was "I reckon she's a mighty fine sort, that lady; she's almost like a mother. Why, she even went to feel if the water was cold for us!"

One day, as I stood by the kitchen steps, she said to me, "Do you remember this place in the old days? The first time you were here?"

She had never alluded to that time before, and all I could think of saying in reply was yes—indeed I remembered it.

"You drove me to the parsonage on one occasion," she said.

I began to entertain fancies that she was by no means

averse to talking with me a little by way of amusement. And I wanted to help her, to make it easier for her to get going; I was also, I guess, rather touched. I answered, "Yes, I remember. It was a glorious drive; only the last part was rather cold for Madame."

"No, it was you who were cold," she replied; "you'd lent me your own blanket from the box. Poor you!"

I was still more touched by this; but then, of course, I had to start giving myself airs—so she hadn't entirely forgotten me! The handful of years since then couldn't have told on me all that severely!

"I think Madame's memory must be mistaken about the blanket," I said; "but we ate in a cottage, and an old woman made coffee for us, and you gave me food."

I put my arms around a post and leaned against the handrail.

This may have offended her, by suggesting I was all set for a prolonged gossip with her; furthermore, I had said, "We ate in a cottage." I had gone too far, of course; but I had grown unused to watching my step, after all those months of wandering.

As soon as I sensed her displeasure, I straightened up, but by then it was too late. That is to say, she was still kindly enough, but the bad days she had fallen on must have made her hypersensitive and suspicious, so that she found discourtesy even in clumsiness.

"Ah yes," she said. "Well, I hope you like it as much at Øvrebø now as you did then."

And with that she nodded and walked away.

Several days passed. The Captain was still away, but Madame had received a friendly postcard from him: he hoped to be home again next week. Also, he was sending pipes, faucets, and cement for the water installation.

"Look!" said Madame, coming to me with the card. "The Captain's sending these things for you and asking you to have them fetched from the station."

We stood there, the two of us, at noon in the middle of the courtyard, reading the card. I can't explain it, but standing there right beside her, with my head inclined toward hers, made me feel good in my inmost being. When she had finished reading she looked up at me. She was playing no game this time; yet, aware as she must have been of a new expression on my face, she continued to look at me. Did she feel my presence as I felt hers? Those two heavy eyes, raised toward mine and held there, were loaded to the brim with love. She could not be held to account: that gaze welled up from pathological depths, blending on its way with the life she carried under her heart. She began breathing heavily, her face flushed dark all over; then she turned on her heel and walked slowly away.

I stood with the card in my hand. Had she given it to me? Had I taken it?

"Your card," I said. "Here, I'm coming…"

She held out her hand behind her without turning around, and walked slowly on.

This incident haunted me for several days. Should I have followed her when she walked away? I could have tried, I could have had a shot; her door was not far away. Pathological? But why had she brought me that card in the first place? She could simply have told me its drift. And now I recalled how six years ago we had stood in just the same way, reading a telegram that the Captain had sent her. Did she seek these situations? And did they do her good?

The next time I saw her I detected no trace of embarrassment; she was friendly and reserved. Better drop the whole business. What did I want with her in any case? Really!

Some callers came one day: a neighbor and her daughter.

They had doubtless heard that the Captain was away and wanted to give his wife some diversion; perhaps, too, they had come from curiosity. Mrs. Falkenberg received them hospitably, was her old amiable self with them, and ended by playing for them on her piano. When they left, she accompanied them down to the road, making sensible conversation, although she must have had other things in her head than domestic economy and slaughtering. How nice and interested she was! "Come again soon—you, Sophie, at the very least." "Thank you, I'd love to. But aren't you ever coming over to Nedrebø again?" "Me? If it hadn't been so late I'd have come with you now." "Well, there's always tomorrow." "Yes, I might well come over to-morrow. Oh, are you there?"—this to Ragnhild, who had followed her down with a shawl. "You really make me laugh, thinking I'm cold. "

All in all, there was a better atmosphere about the place; that sense of malaise no longer weighed on us all. Grindhusen and I worked away at our famous reservoir, and Lars Falkenberg came farther and farther uphill with his trench. Seeing the Captain was away so long, I was keen to push ahead in the hope of getting most of the work completed by the time he returned; what a lark it would be if we got the whole thing done! He could do with a nice little surprise, because—well, yes, there had indeed been conflict the night before he left. Something may have reminded him of the calamity afflicting his home; perhaps an unburned book still lying around in his wife's room. His last words had been, "Well, now I'm felling timber to pay that debt;

and the harvest will bring in a lot of money, too. So I hope the Lord will forgive me—as I forgive him. Good night, Louise !"

When we had laid the last stone of the reservoir and cemented the whole thing, Grindhusen and I joined forces with Lars for the last of the digging. It went with a will. Here and there a boulder needed blasting, here and there a tree had to come down; but the trench crept up and up, until finally there was a long black line all the way from the reservoir to the manor. Then we worked our way back, digging down to the right depth. Naturally the trench was not intended as a work of art; rather as an underground resting place for some water pipes that needed burying without delay. It was merely a question of getting below the deep-frost level, and of getting there before the frost set in. It was already coating the fields at night. Nils dropped all his other work in order to help us.

Building or digging, however, I was using only my hands; and my mind in its idleness toyed with all manner of notions. Each time I remembered the postcard incident, it sent a glow all through me. Yes, but why give it another thought? Really! Besides, I hadn't followed her to the door, had I?

But there was she, and there were you. Her breath

was on you, you tasted flesh. She came from some darkness—she was certainly not of this earth. Remember the eyes?

And each time the glow was followed by a wave of nausea. Into my mind would pour a meaningless succession of wild and tender names of places she might have come from: Uganda, Antananarivo, Honolulu, Venezuela, Atacama. Was it verse? Were they colors? I could make nothing of them.


# XIII

Madame ordered the carriage; she needed to go to the station. She seemed in no great hurry: she told the cook to prepare some food for the journey, and when Nils asked if she wanted the calash or the landau, she thought for a moment before choosing the landau and pair.

Then off she went, driven by Nils himself.

That same evening they were home again, having turned back when halfway there.

Had Madame forgotten something? Now she demanded fresh horses and another hamper of food; she intended to leave again at once. Nils objected that night was coming on, that they would be driving in the dark;

but Madame repeated her order. While she waited she sat in the living room with her things on, doing nothing—she had not forgotten anything—just sitting there, staring. Ragnhild went in and asked if she could help with anything. No, thank you. Madame sat leaning forward, as if bowed down with some mortal sorrow.

The carriage was ready; Madame came out.

On seeing Nils all set to drive again, she took pity on him and said that Grindhusen should drive her. While waiting for Grindhusen, she sat on the steps.

Then off they drove. It was a fine evening, pleasantly cool for the horses.

"I can't make it out," said Nils; "she's a changed person. I had no idea of anything until she knocked on the glass and told me to turn back; we were about halfway. But she never said a word about wanting to go straight out again."

"Surely she must have forgotten something."

"Ragnhild says no. She was in the living room, and I wondered about those photographs, whether she was going to take them and burn them; but no, they're still there. All the time she was back she never did a single thing."

I crossed the yard with Nils, who continued, "No, there's something very wrong with Madame; she's got no harmony left for anything. Where do you suppose she's off to now? Heaven knows—she hardly seemed to know her own mind. We stopped to rest the horses and she said, 'I'm so busy, Nils, there's so many places I ought to be at the same time, and I shouldn't be away from home either.' 'Madame shouldn't be so busy,' I said; 'Madame should just take things easy.' But you know how she is these days—you can't say anything to her. She just looked at her watch and said we must be off again."

"Was this on the way to the station?"

"No, on the way home just now. She seemed almost more edgy then."

"Perhaps the Captain's written for her to join him?"

Nils shook his head.

"No. Or rather, heaven knows. By the way, tomorrow's Sunday, isn't it?"

"Yes?"

"Oh, nothing really. It's just that I want to use the day working out a route for fetching firewood in the winter. I've had it in mind for some time. It's easier now than when the snow's on the ground."

Nils had the running of the place constantly in mind. It was a matter of honor; and now, in addition, he was anxious to show himself grateful for the handsome increase the Captain had given him since the harvest.

Sunday.

I took a stroll up the hill, and inspected the reservoir and trench. A few more good days and we would have the pipe laid. I was all keyed up and could hardly wait for Sunday to be over before returning to the attack. The Captain, moreover, had never meddled in my project by as much as a single word, but had left me completely in charge, so to me it was by no means a matter of indifference if the frost came and spoiled things for us.

When I got back, there was the landau standing in the courtyard; but the horses had been unhitched. It was more or less the time when Grindhusen was due back; but why had he pulled up by the front steps? I went into the kitchen.

The maids came running to me: Madame was sitting in the landau; she had come home a second time. She had been all the way to the station; now she wanted to go there again. What did I make of it all?

"Must be her nerves," I said. "Where's Nils?"

"Up in the forest. He said he'd be out for quite a while. There's only us here, and we can't say more to her than we've said already."

"And where's Grindhusen?"

"Gone to change the horses again. And Madame just sits in the carriage and won't get out. Do go and talk to her."

"Well, it's not all that serious if she goes for a drive or two. So take it easy."

I went out to Madame, my heart beating fast. How completely she had gone to pieces, how hopeless everything must seem to her! I opened the carriage door, bowed, and said, "Will Madame allow me to drive her this time?"

She looked at me calmly and said, "No, why?"

"Grindhusen may be a bit tired—I don't know—"

"He promised to drive me," she said. "No, he's not tired. Is he coming soon?"

"I don't see him," I answered.

"Shut this door again, and go and tell him to come," she commanded, wrapping herself more closely as she spoke.

I went across to the stables, where Grindhusen was harnessing the fresh horses.

"What's up?" I asked. "Are you off again somewhere?"

"Yes? Aren't I?" said Grindhusen, breaking off for a moment.

"It all looks very odd to me. Where's Madame going—do you know?"

"No. She wanted to come straight back from the station last night, but I said neither of us could stand it. So she slept at the hotel. But this morning she still wanted to go home, or so she said. And now she wants to go to the station again, she says. I don't know."

He continued harnessing.

"Madame told me to hurry you up," I said.

"All right, I'm coming now. But these bellybands are the devil's own work."

"Aren't you too tired to make that journey again?"

"No, I dare say I'll manage it. And she's given me quite a bit extra."

"Has she, indeed?"

"Sure. Oh yes, she's a mighty nice creature."

Then I said to Grindhusen, "I don't think you ought to start off again now."

He broke off abruptly. "You think not? No, perhaps you're right."

At this point Madame called, from just outside the stable door, "What, aren't you ready yet? How much longer am I to sit there waiting for you?"

"I'm coming this minute!" Grindhusen answered, and set to work more busily than ever. "It was only these bellybands."

Madame ran back to the landau. The thick fur coat she had on was too heavy for her, and she flailed with her arms to keep her balance. There was something pathetic in the sight—like a hen trying to escape across a barnyard and flapping its wings to help.

209

I went over to Madame again; I was polite, indeed humble; I took off my cap and begged her to give up this new journey.

"You're not driving me," she answered.

"No. But if Madame would make up her mind to stay at home…"

But now she took offense. She measured me, inspected me, and said, "Excuse me, but you're not to meddle in this. Even if I did get you dismissed once—"

"No no, it's not that!" I said despairingly, and was lost for words. When she took that line she reduced me to pulp.

For one moment a paroxysm of rage seized me: I had only to reach into the carriage and lift out this child, this pitiful hen! My arms must have twitched, for she gave a frightened start and shifted her position. Then suddenly reaction set in; I turned soft and foolish, and embarked on another attempt.

"It's so cheerless when you're away—we all feel it. Can't we find something here to amuse you with instead—I can read a little, read aloud a little, and of course Lars sings beautifully. And perhaps I can tell stories—one thing or another. Grindhusen's coming now—shall I send him away again?"

She seemed mollified, and thought for a moment. Then she said, "I think you must have got it all wrong.

I'm going to meet the Captain. He didn't come the day before yesterday, and he didn't come yesterday, but sooner or later he's bound to come. I want to go and meet him."

"Oh!"

"So be off with you. Is Grindhusen there?"

I felt as if I had been struck across the mouth. She was right, it sounded so plausible—and oh, I had made a fool of myself again!

"Yes, Grindhusen's here," I managed to get out.

And I put my cap on again and even helped Grindhusen hitch the horses. I was so bewildered and shamefaced that I didn't even offer an apology, but could only flutter this way and that, checking the harness all over.

"So it's you who's driving me, Grindhusen?" called Madame.

"What, me? Why, sure!" he answered.

Then she slammed the door to, and the landau rolled out of the yard.

"Has she gone?" asked the maids, clasping their hands.

"Certainly she's gone. She's going to meet her husband."

I went back up to the reservoir. With Grindhusen

away, the team was a man short; could the rest of us manage the extra work?

But it had already dawned on me that Mrs. Falkenberg had caught me off guard with that trumped-up story about going to meet her husband. Not that it mattered: the horses were thoroughly rested, having done no work while Nils was helping us with the trench. All the same, I had behaved stupidly. Why couldn't I have got up on the box myself, without asking permission? Yes, and then? Well, in that case any subsequent follies would to some extent have been channeled through me, and I might have been able to stop them. Ha-ha—you infatuated old man! Madame must have known what she intended: to get her own back on the Captain and be away when he returned. She vacillated endlessly, kept wanting to and not wanting to, wanting to and not wanting to; but the intention was there. And bless my soul, I had not set out on my wanderings for the sole purpose of looking after the bourgeois interests of married couples involved in love affairs. Their pigeon! But how corrupt Mrs. Falkenberg had become! She had indeed received an injury, an injury tantamount to her destruction: she no longer cared what she did to herself. And she had taken to lying. After the cabaret eyes, the pack of lies: the white lie today, the compulsive lie tomorrow, one leading to the other. But where would it end? Life could afford to waste her, to fritter her away.

We worked on the trench for another three days, till we had only a few yards left. There were now up to five or six degrees of frost at night, but this did not prevent us from pressing steadily forward. Grindhusen had returned and been set to work digging a tunnel for the pipe under the kitchen; I myself dug under the barn and stables as being the most important. Meanwhile, Nils and Lars Falkenberg were putting the finishing touches to the trench.

On the third day I at last questioned Grindhusen about Madame. "So she didn't come home with you again that last time? "

"No, she took the train."

"It was her husband she was going to join, was it?"

But Grindhusen had become extremely wary of me; for two days he had never opened his mouth, and now he only said, "That's about what it comes to, I should say. Well, yes, I suppose so—her own husband, you understand…"

"I thought perhaps she might have been going to her parents in Kristiansand."

"Yes, maybe, maybe," said Grindhusen, finding this an improvement. "Gee, it's as clear as day she's gone there for a while. Well, I dare say she'll be home again soon."

"Did she say she would?"

"Sounded like that, yes. Though the Captain hasn't come home yet either, for that matter. Yes, she's a mighty fine woman. She says to me, 'Here's something for food and drink for you and the horses—and here's something extra,' she says. Ah, you won't find another such mistress."

But Grindhusen felt safer with the maids; and to them he had said it was a toss-up whether Madame would be coming home again. She had quizzed him about Engineer Lassen all the way, and had certainly gone to stay with him. Ah, that was a man she wouldn't go disappearing from—not with his wealth and splendor!

Then came another postcard from the Captain to his wife, just to ask if she would please get Nils to meet him at the station on Friday, and to bring his fur coat without fail. The card had been delayed; Friday meant tomorrow. Incidentally, it was fortunate on this occasion that Ragnhild had happened to take a squint at the message side of the card.

We sat in Nils's room talking about the Captain, wondering what his reaction would be when he got home, what we should say, whether indeed we should say anything. All three maids were present at this conclave. There was comfortable time for Madame to have reached Christiania by the time the Captain wrote her that card; since she had evidently not done so, she must have been going elsewhere. The whole thing was sad beyond words.

Nils asked, "Didn't she leave any letter?"

But no such letter was lying about. As against that, Ragnhild had, on her own initiative, done something which perhaps she oughtn't: she had taken those photographs off the piano and thrown them in the stove. Was that wrong?

"No, Ragnhild, indeed not."

She also told us she had gone through Madame's things and sorted out all the handkerchiefs that weren't hers. Oh, and she had found various things in her room—a purse with Hugo Lassen's initials embroidered on it, a book with his name in full, some sweets in an envelope with his address on—and had burned the lot.

Ragnhild really was an extraordinary girl. What an instinct! A case of the devil turned monk? After making such heavy use of the red stair carpet and all those keyholes.

For myself and my work, it fitted like a glove that the Captain had not demanded transport until this moment. The trench was now complete over its entire length; and for laying pipes I could dispense with Nils.

On the other hand, when it came to covering them up, I would need every man jack. The weather, by the way, had turned mild and rainy, with the temperature well above freezing.

It was doubtless an excellent thing for me at this period that I had the water installation to hold my interest: it saved me, probably, from many a mad caprice. From time to time I would clench my fists in pain, and when I found myself alone at the reservoir, I was liable to stand and scream at the forest; but there was no chance of my getting away. Besides, where would I go?

The Captain was back.

Without even taking off his fur coat or snow boots, he went all around the house: in the living room, in the kitchen, in all the upstairs rooms, then down again.

"Where's the mistress?" he asked.

"The mistress went to meet the Captain," answered Ragnhild. "We expected her by now."

The Captain's head began to droop. Feeling his way, he said, "You mean, she drove down with Nils to the station? But how maddening that I didn't look for her more carefully!"

Ragnhild said, "No, Madame left on Sunday."

The Captain took a fresh grip on himself and said, "Sunday. So she must have been going to meet me in

Christiania. Hm. We've missed each other: as it happens, I made a little side trip yesterday, to Drammen—I mean Fredrikstad. Have you got any food for me, Ragahild?"

"It's on the table, sir, if you please."

"Come to think of it, it was the day before yesterday I made that side trip. Well, at least she'll have had a little outing! Everything all right here? Men busy digging that trench?"

"They've finished it, I believe."

The Captain went in.

And Ragnhild came running to us at once and repeating every word, to give us something to go by, and to save us from making bad worse.

Later on the Captain came out to see us, greeting us officer-style with "How's it going, boys?" He was amazed to find the pipes all laid; indeed, we had already started covering them over.

"Splendid fellows!" he exclaimed. "You don't take as long over a job as I do!"

With that he left us and went up to the reservoir. When he came back he was less keen-eyed, more withdrawn; perhaps he had been sitting there in solitude, thinking various thoughts. Now he stood watching us, one hand on his chin. After a moment or two he said to Nils, "Well, I've sold the timber."

"Dare say the Captain got a good price for it too?"

"Yes, I did. A good price. But I've taken all this time over it. You've been quicker here."

"Ah, but there've been several of us on this job," I said. "Sometimes as many as four."

He tried to make a joke. "Oh yes, I know you're an extravagant man to have around."

But there was no mirth in his face, and his smile hardly deserved the name. He was flagging now, with a vengeance. After a while he sat down on a stone we'd removed from the trench—it was covered with fresh clay; and from this position he followed us with his eyes.

Feeling sorry for his poor clothes, I went up to him, spade in hand, and said, "Shall I scrape some of the clay off that stone?"

"No, it doesn't matter."

All the same, he got up and allowed me to clean it a little.

At that moment Ragnhild came running along the trench toward us. She had something white in her hand, a piece of paper. And she ran and ran. The Captain sat watching her.

"It's only a telegram," she said breathlessly. "It came express. "

The Captain got up and took a few quick steps toward this telegram. Then he tore it open and read it.

We could see at once it must be something serious: the Captain gave a great gasp. Then he made for the house, at a walk, at a run; a short way off he turned and shouted to Nils, "The carriage, at once! I'm going to the station."

Then he ran on again.

And the Captain set out once more. He had only been home a matter of hours.

Ragnhild told us how jittery the poor man had been: trying to get into the carriage without his fur coat, forgetting the hamper of food prepared for him, leaving the telegram wide open on the stairs.

ACCIDENT, it said…YOUR WIFE…CHIEF OF PO-LICE. "What's it all about?"

"I thought as much when it came express," Ragnhild said in an unfamiliar voice; then she turned away. "I've a strong feeling it's a terrible accident."

"No, surely," I said, reading and rereading. "Look, it's not so serious—listen to this: REQUEST YOUR IM-MEDIATE PRESENCE, ACCIDENT INVOLVING YOUR WIFE. CHIEF OF POLICE.

It was an express telegram from the little town, the dead town. Yes, that was it. A town with a roar right through it—a long bridge—rapids. All screams died on the screamer's lips; no one heard them. And no birds sang…

But all the maids were coming and talking to me in unfamiliar voices; misery reigned supreme among us. So I had to be grave and confident. "Madame must have fallen and hurt herself; she hasn't been too steady on her feet of late. But I dare say she picked herself up again and walked off hardly the worse for it—just a little bleeding. They're too hasty sending telegrams, these police chiefs."

"No, that's not true," said Ragnhild. "You know very well that if the Chief of Police sends a telegram, it probably means that Madame's been found dead somewhere. Oh, I can't—I just can't—bear it…"

They were evil days that followed. I worked harder than ever before, but like a sleepwalker, without interest and without pleasure. Was the Captain never coming?

Three days later he came, silent and alone. The body had been sent to Kristiansand; he had only come home to change his clothes before following it there, to the funeral.

This time he was home for at most an hour; then off again, to catch the morning train. I never even saw him, being out in the grounds.

Ragnhild asked if he had seen his wife alive.

He looked at her and frowned.

But the girl refused to give up—she begged him,

please, in God's name, to say. And the two other girls stood behind her, equally despairing.

Then the Captain answered—in a voice so low that he seemed to be speaking only to himself—"She had been dead for several days when I got there. It was an accident—she tried to cross the river and the ice was too thin. No, there was no ice; it was the stones that were slippery. Or rather, there was ice as well."

And now the girls set up a wailing; but this was too much for the Captain. He got up from his chair, cleared his throat hard, and said, "There, there—all right, girls, you must go now. Wait, Ragnhild!" And what he had to say to her in private was this: "By the way, is it you who's taken down some photographs from the piano? I can't make out where they've got to."

Then Ragnhild recovered her wits and answered gloriously—God bless her for the lie—"Me? No, it was Madame took them down one day."

"So. Well, well. It's just that I was puzzled by their having gone."

It helped—helped the Captain, this enlightenment.

As he left, he told Ragnhild to say I was not to leave Øvrebø before he returned.

# XIV

No, I did not go away.

I worked, trudged through the dreariest days of my life to their end, and got the water installation completed. It made a bit of a change the first time we were able to turn on the water, and we all felt better for having something new to talk about for a while.

Lars Falkenberg had left us now. All differences between him and me were finally resolved; it was just as in the old days when we wandered around the countryside together.

He was better off than many another man: his heart was light, his head empty, and his health immutably sound. To be sure, his singing days down at the manor were gone forever; but he himself had evidently come in later years to mistrust his voice a little, and now he merely larded his speech with tales of how at one time—in his day—he used to sing at dances and before the gentry. No, for Lars Falkenberg things were not too bad—he had his little patch of earth with two cows and a pig, not to mention his wife and children.

But what were Grindhusen and I to do? I could wander off anywhere, but the good Grindhusen was incapable of wandering. He was only fit for staying put in one place after another and working until he was fired. And each time the harsh announcement came, he had grown so flabby that he took it very hard and thought it was mighty tough on him. After a while, however, he regained his confidence and his childhood faith—not in himself but in destiny, in providence, saying in his shiftless way, "Ah well, with God's help something will turn up."

But he too was well enough off. He had a unique gift for making the best of every place he came to, and could happily stay there till he died if the choice rested with him. Home was a place he never needed to go: his children were grown up, his wife managed nicely without him. No, this old, red-haired firebrand of yesteryear needed nothing now but a place to lay his head and use his hands.

"Where are you going from here?" he asked me.

"Far away up in the mountains, to Trovatn, to a forest."

And for all his total disbelief he said, quietly and evasively, "Maybe, maybe."

After we had finished the plumbing, Grindhusen and I were set to work on the firewood until the Captain returned. We cut up and stacked the top ends the loggers had left—nice, steady work.

"I'll bet you we're both laid off when the Captain gets back," said Grindhusen.

"You could get work here for the winter," I suggested. "Out of these thousand dozen battens there'll be a mass of cordwood left, which you could saw up for a reasonable wage."

"Yes—speak to the Captain about it, will you?"

And now the hope of a long spell of work for the winter made this man a contented soul again. Grindhusen was good at enduring his own company. Grindhusen, therefore, was by no means badly off.

That left me. And alas, I found my own company was scarcely to be endured a moment longer.

That Sunday I loitered here and loitered there: I was waiting for the Captain, who was expected home that day. Then, just in case, I went for a long walk up along the stream that fed our reservoir; I wanted to see once again the two little pools of water up on the hillside, the sources of the Nile.

On my way down through the woods, I met Lars Falkenberg on his way up, going home. The full moon was just rising, red and enormous, and lighting up the whole landscape. There had also been a little snow and frost; the air was easy to breathe. Lars was as friendly as could be; he had been drinking brandy somewhere, and now talked fifteen to the dozen. But I would not have chosen to meet him.

I had stood for a long time up on the hillside, listening to the sough from heaven and earth; there was nothing else to be heard. Then there might come a rustling sound, which would prove to be a shriveled, curled-up leaf fluttering down through the frozen branches; it was like listening to a tiny fountain. Then heaven and earth would sough again. A mildness enveloped me, as though all my strings were muted.

Lars Falkenberg wanted to know where I had been and where I was going. Stream? Reservoir? A load of monkey business the whole caboodle—as if people couldn't carry water for themselves. The Captain had gone in for so many newfangled inventions and plowing among the crops and suchlike paraphernalia, he'd come a cropper one fine day. A rich harvest it was supposed to be. Fair enough. But they never stopped to consider the cost, with a machine for every blessed thing, and several men to each machine. Imagine what Grindhusen and I must have cost this summer! What he himself must have cost this autumn, for that matter! In the old days there had been music and plenty at Øvrebø, and a certain person had been in the living room and sung—"I don't care to talk about it," said Lars. "And soon there won't be a decent stick of timber in the forest."

"And in a few years it'll be as thick as ever."

"A few years? Years and years, if you ask me. No sirree, it's not just a matter of being a Captain and shouting *Hut-two-three*—and hey presto, Bob's your uncle. And he's not even spokesman for the district any longer, and you never see a soul coming to ask his advice on everything under the sun—"

"Did you see the Captain down at Øvrebø? Is he back yet?" I interrupted.

"Just back, and looking like a skeleton. What was I going to say…When are you leaving?"

"Tomorrow."

"Tomorrow already!" Lars was full of goodwill and all-the-best toward me; he had never dreamed I'd be off so soon.

"Well, in that case it's a toss-up if I'll see you again this time," he said. "But there's one thing I don't mind telling you: it's time you stopped frittering away your life and never settling down anywhere. I'm saying this for the last time now—so don't you forget, mind. It's not that I'm all that well off; but how many of the likes of us have done better, I'd like to know—certainly not you. I do at least have a roof over my head, and that's a fact. Wife and kids, two cows—one to calve in the spring, the other in autumn—and a pig, and that's as much as I possess in the world. Nothing to boast about—but it all adds up to a farm, such as it is."

"It's all right for a chap like you who's come out on top," I said.

Lars grew still more friendly at this acknowledgment; he positively overflowed with goodwill toward me.

"I don't know anyone who could be more on top than you, for that matter," he continued. "You're good at all sorts of work, and writing and doing sums into the bargain. But it's your own stupid fault. You could have done as I told you six or seven years ago and taken one of the girls here like I took Emma and settled down for good. Then you wouldn't be traipsing around now from parish to parish. And that's what I'd still advise you to do."

"It's too late now," I answered.

"Yes, you've gone hideously gray, so I don't know who'd have you now from around these parts. How old are you?"

"Really, what a question to ask!"

"Well, you'd hardly be a chicken exactly, still. There was something I meant to say—come up my way for a stretch, maybe it'll come back to me."

I went with him, talking all the way. He offered to put in a good word for me with the Captain, so that I too could get a clearing in the forest.

"Well, that really is funny," he said, "my forgetting so completely what I had in mind. Come on home with me now, and it's bound to come back."

He was goodwill incarnate. But I had one or two things to sort out and didn't feel like accompanying him any farther.

"You won't see the Captain tonight in any case."

No, but it was getting late; Emma must have gone to bed; I would only be disturbing her.

"Not a bit of it!" said Lars. "If she's gone to bed, well then, she's gone to bed. I wouldn't be surprised, either, if there isn't a shirt of yours still lying around at our place. Come and take it with you, and save Emma going all that way with it."

"No, I'd better not—but remember me to Emma," I ventured to say now.

"Shall do. And if you really haven't got time to come up to my little place, such as it is—are you leaving early in the morning?"

Forgetting that I wouldn't be able to see the Captain that evening, I said yes, I'd be leaving first thing.

"In that case I'll send Emma down with that shirt of yours this instant," said Lars. "And goodbye for now! Don't forget what I've told you!"

And so we parted.

When I had gone a little way, I slackened off speed: there was really no great hurry about my packing and other preparations. I turned and set off uphill again, whistling in the moonlight. It was a lovely evening, no hint of cold, only a soft, compliant peace enveloping the woods. After half an hour or so I was surprised to find Emma on her way with my shirt.

Next morning neither Grindhusen nor I went out in the woods. Grindhusen was uneasy and asked, "Have you spoken to the Captain about me?"

"No, I haven't spoken to him at all."

"No, you mark my words, he's going to lay me off. If there was any go in him, he'd let me chop up that cordwood; but not him! It's about as much as he can do to keep a man at all."

"What's all this, Grindhusen? Surely you liked Captain Falkenberg well enough before?"

"Yes, you know that. Well, yes, that's to say, the man may be all right. Hm…I can't help wondering if the Inspector of Log Driving mightn't find some job or other for me to do now. He's a very effluent man, you know, that inspector…"

At eight o'clock I managed to see the Captain, and talked with him for a while; then a couple of neighbors called, doubtless to offer their condolences. The Captain looked strained but by no means crushed, his bearing was steadfast and straightforward. He questioned me a little about a plan of his for a big drying house for hay and grain.

And now, it seemed, there was no more disorder at

Øvrebø, no agitation of the mind, no derailed soul! I thought of this almost with melancholy. No one placed impertinent photographs on the piano, but no one played the piano either. It stood there, dumb, since the last note died away. No, Mrs. Falkenberg was no longer here to injure herself or others. Of the old days nothing was left. It only remained to be seen whether Øvrebø would be strewn with happiness and flowers forever after.

"As long as he doesn't take to drink again," I said to Nils.

"No, surely," he replied. "And I don't think he ever really took to drink. He was just a bit foolish, I'd say, living it up the way he did for a time. To change the subject—are you coming back in the spring?"

"No, I shall never come back again now."

So Nils and I said our farewells. I wanted to fix in my memory the man's equanimity and honorable way of thinking, and stood watching as he walked away across the yard. Then he turned and said, "Were you in the woods yesterday? Is there enough snow for me to use the sleigh getting firewood today?"

"Yes," I said.

His mind set at ease, he went to the stables to harness up.

Then Grindhusen in turn passed me on his way to

the stables. He stopped for a moment to tell me that the Captain had, of his own free will, offered him work cutting firewood. "'Saw up as much of that cordwood as you can,' he says; 'just carry on for the time being—I'm sure we'll agree all right about wages.' 'My thanks and respects, Captain,' says I. 'Go and report to Nils,' says he. Ah, what a fine fellow! You won't find many like him."

Shortly afterward I was sent for by the Captain, and went up to his office. He thanked me for my work, both indoors and out, and paid me my wages. That just about finished our business; but he asked me one or two questions about the proposed drying house, and we talked it over for a while. It would all have to wait till after Christmas, in any case, he said; but when the time came he would be glad to have me back. As he said this he looked at me; then he added, "But I suppose you're never coming back now?"

I was taken by surprise. But I met his gaze and answered, "That's correct."

On my way down I turned his words over in my mind. Had he seen through me? At all events, he had trusted me in a way that I valued highly. He was a real gentleman.

Trusted me? But what had it cost him? I belonged to the ranks of the superannuated. He had allowed me to go and do and pretend as I pleased, all on the strength of my eminent harmlessness. That must be it. In any case, there was nothing to see through.

I went all around the house, upstairs and downstairs, taking my leave of one and all, of Ragnhild and the girls. Then, as I crossed the courtyard with my knapsack on my shoulder, Captain Falkenberg called from the steps, "It's just occurred to me—if you're going to the station, the lad can drive you."

Ever the gentleman! But I thanked him and declined the offer. I didn't feel so superannuated but that I could manage that stretch on foot.


And now I was back in my little town again. I had come here on my way to Trovatn and the mountains.

Here everything was as before, except that a thin layer of ice now covered the river above and below the rapids, and the ice was coated with snow.

I kept a weather eye open and bought some clothes and equipment, and after picking up a good pair of new shoes, I took the old pair to the cobbler to get them half-soled. The cobbler chatted a while, then begged me to be so good as to be seated. "And where's himself from, now?" he asked. And at once I was soaked in the spirit of the place.

I sauntered up to the churchyard. Here, too, they

were keeping a weather eye open and preparing for winter. Bundles of straw had been lashed around plants and bushes, many a delicate tombstone was crowned with a high wooden hat; while the hats themselves had been protected with paint. It was as if people had said to themselves: Look, I own this tombstone now—with care and foresight it can serve as a tombstone for me and my kith and kin for many generations.

There was a Christmas fair on, too, and here in turn I sauntered. There were toboggans and skis, wooden butter dishes from the nether regions and subterranean chairs carved from logs, rose-colored mittens, clothes mangles, fox skins. And then there were horse dealers and cattle dealers mingling with drunken folk from up the valley; yes, and Jews who had come to palm off an ornamented pocket watch or two, in this town that had no money. And the watches came from that country up in the Alps where Böcklin was at pains *not* to come from, where nobody and nothing ever came from.*

Oh, this Christmas market of ours!

---

\* Arnold Böcklin (1827–1901), at one time an immensely popular painter who peopled his romantic landscapes with classical nymphs and satyrs, was born and died in Switzerland but lived most of his life abroad.—Trans.

But the evenings offered noble entertainment for all: dancing in two large halls, virtuoso performances on the Hardanger fiddle, and eh but it's grand—that's about long and short on't. The Hardanger fiddle has iron strings, it produces no melodious phrases, it is music with a sting in it. It affects different people in different ways: some of us soak it up with national mawkishness, others of us bare our teeth and howl with melancholy. Never was such a powerful effect produced by stinging music.

And the dance went on.

Poor aged mother, toiling hard,
Spending your sweat like blood,

sang the local schoolmaster during an interval. But some of the wilder lads wanted dancing and nothing but. What was all this? Stand about with your arm around a girl, *singing?* No sense in that! The singer broke off. "What, no sense in Vinje?" Dancing versus the poet Vinje. Argument for and against, yelling and screaming, uproar. Never was such a powerful effect produced by poetry and singing.

And the dance went on.

The lasses from up the valley were five pink petticoats thick; but this counted for nothing with such experienced bearers as these. And the dance went on, and the thunder went on, and the brandy was potent, and a steam arose from the witches' caldron. At three in the morning the local police force appeared and banged on the floor with its baton. Period. The dancers went out in the moonlight and spread out over the town and its environs. And nine months later the lasses from up the valley produced conclusive evidence that they had still been one pink petticoat short. Never was such a powerful effect produced by the want of one pink petticoat.

The river had grown quieter now—not much of a river to look at; winter had mantled it over. It still drove the pulp mills and sawmills along its banks, because it was and remained a great river—but a river with no life in it, a river that had shut the lid on itself.

As for the rapids, they too were in poor shape. Once I had gazed down at them and listened to them and thought: If I lived down there in the world of that roar forever, what in the end would become of my brain? Now the rapids were shrunk and murmured meekly; it would have been a mockery to speak of a roar. Dear God, the rapids were in utter ruin! They had sunk into poverty; great boulders stuck out all along the bank, logs had wedged themselves at all kinds of angles; one could jump dry-shod from bank to bank, by way of stone and timber.

And now I stood with my knapsack on, having finished my business in the town. It was Sunday; the weather was fine and clear.

I went to the hotel and announced myself to the underporter. The great, good-natured creature wanted to come with me up along the river for part of the way, and also to carry my knapsack—as if I couldn't carry it myself.

We followed the right-hand bank, although the road proper was on the left; ours was only a summer path trodden by log drivers, and showing now a few fresh tracks in the snow. My guide couldn't quite make out why we didn't follow the road; he was not strong in the head. But I had already been up this way twice in the last few days, and wanted to do so once again. It was my own tracks we could see the whole way.

I asked, "The lady you mentioned once—the one who got drowned—was it about here?"

"The one who fell in, eh? Ay, we're just about there. It was terrible; in the end there must have been twenty of us searching for her—police and all."

"Did you drag the river?"

"Ay, we dragged it. Laid planks and ladders down—stood on 'em—crack! Broke up nearly all the ice that way. Here, you can see where we went," he added, stopping.

I made out the dark stretch of ice where the boats had rowed around, crushing the ice and dragging; now it had frozen over again.

The underporter went on with his story. "We found her in the end. I must say, it was a blessing the river was so low. She'd gone straight to the bottom between two rocks and stuck there. There was no current to speak of; if it had been in the spring, she'd have gone for miles."

"So she thought she'd cross the river?"

"Ay, they all want to go out on the ice the moment it freezes over; it's asking for trouble. Someone had been across already—two days earlier, it was. She came walking along, just here, this side we're on now, and the engineer he came down the road on the other side—he'd been out on his bicycle. Then they saw one another and signaled to each other—just saying hello or something of the kind, because they were related together, both of them. But then the lady mistook one of the signals, so the engineer says, and thought he was beckoning to her, because she started to cross. And the engineer he yelled, but she didn't hear, and he had his bicycle, which he couldn't leave—and, in any case, somebody had been across already. The engineer told the police about how it all happened and they wrote down every word. Well, then when she was halfway across, down she went. She must have happened to tread on a really rotten part of the ice. And the engineer he came flashing through the town on his bicycle, back to the hotel, and started ringing. I've never heard such ringing in all my days. 'Someone's fallen in the river!' he shouted. 'My cousin!' he shouted. We all turned out, the engineer too. We had ropes and boat hooks with us, but it was no use; then the police came, and the fire brigade came, and they got hold of a boat somewhere up there carried it between them till they reached us, then they got it out and started dragging. But we didn't find her, not the first day we didn't. But then the second day we found her. Ay, it was a nasty accident, that."

"Did you say her husband came—the Captain?"

"Ay, the Captain came. And you can imagine the state he was in—though to tell you the truth we all were, for that matter—the whole town. As for the engineer, he was quite beside himself for a long time, they said at the hotel, and when the Captain came, the engineer went off inspecting up the river; he just couldn't bear to talk about the accident any more."

"So the Captain never saw him?"

"No. Hm. Well, I don't rightly know." He looked around him. "No, I don't really know at all."

His answer was so shifty that I realized he *did* know something. But it was of no significance, and I refrained from questioning him further.

"Well, many thanks for your company," I said, and gave him some money for a winter garment or two. And I said goodbye to him, and wanted him to turn back.

However, he was keen to go on with me a little farther. And to get me to agree to this, he suddenly said: Yes, the Captain *had* got hold of the engineer while he was here. This good, dimwitted soul had understood enough of the maids' gossip in the kitchen to have just about grasped the connection between the engineer and this cousin who came to stay; but that was as far as he got. However, it was he and no other who had guided the Captain up the river in search of the engineer.

"The Captain simply had to meet the engineer," he went on, "and I went with him up the river. 'What is there for the engineer to inspect on an ice-bound river?' the Captain asked me on the way. 'I can't make that out either,' I said. So we walked all day till about three o'clock. 'I wonder if he mightn't be in this cabin,' I said; 'I'm told his men stay here sometimes.' After that, the Captain didn't want me to come any farther—just told me to wait. Then he went up to the cabin and went inside. He'd hardly been gone more than a minute or two, then out he came from the cabin, and the engineer too. They spoke a few words together—I didn't hear what they said. Then all of a sudden the Captain threw up his arm in the air—like that—and fetched the engineer one, so he went flat on his back. Lord bless you, it must have been like an avalanche through his head. And not content with that, the Captain picked the engineer up again and fetched him another great crack. Then he came back to me and said, 'Let's go home now.'"

This set me thinking. I was amazed that the underporter, this man who had no enemies and bore malice to none, should have allowed the engineer to remain at the cabin without help. Nor had he shown a trace of disapproval in his account of the punishment. My guess was that the engineer had been miserly with him too, and had never paid for his services, but only acted the nabob and laughed at him and behaved like a whelp. Yes, that would be it. And perhaps this time it was no longer my jealousy leading me astray.

"But the Captain—he was the lad for giving tips!" concluded the underporter. "I paid off all my debts with what he gave me, I did and all."

When at last I had finally got rid of the underporter, I crossed the river; the ice was firm enough. Then I continued up the road, thinking about his story. That assault at the cabin—what purpose had it served? It settled nothing, beyond the fact that one of the parties was big and strong, while the other was a little runt of a sportsman with a big bottom. Still, the Captain was an officer, who had doubtless remembered vaguely that something of the kind was due. He ought, perhaps, to have remembered vaguely, while there was still time, that other things were due. Who can say? It was his wife who had gone in the river, and whatever the Captain might do now, she would never come back.

But even if she could have, what then? Assuredly, she had been born to her destiny. Both husband and wife had tried to patch up the damage and had failed. I remembered her as she had been six or seven years back: bored and already attracted, no doubt, to this man and that; but faithful and sensitive. Time continued to pass. She had no mission, only three maids in her home. She had no children, only a grand piano. She had no children.

And life can afford to be wasteful.

It was mother and child that went to the bottom.

A wanderer plays on muted strings when he reaches the age of two score years and ten. That is when he plays on muted strings.

Or I might put it like this:

If he comes too late in the autumn to the woods where the berries grow, why then, he comes to them too late; and if one fine day he no longer feels up to making merry and laughing uproariously from *joie de vivre,* why then, it must be because he is old; don't blame him for that! Besides, beyond question, it takes a certain degree of brainlessness to remain permanently contented with oneself and with everything. But favorable moments we all have. A condemned man sits in his tumbril on the way to the scaffold; a nail in the seat irks him; he shifts position and feels more comfortable.

It is wrong of a captain to ask God to forgive him—as he forgives God. He is simply dramatizing. A wanderer who doesn't each day find food and drink, clothes and shoes, house and home provided, according to his needs, feels just the right degree of privation when all these splendors are absent. If one thing doesn't work out, another will. And if that other fails to work out also, he does not go around forgiving God but takes the responsibility himself. He puts his shoulder to the wheel of fortune—that is to say, he bows his back before it. It's a trifle hard on flesh and blood, it grays the hair horribly; but a wanderer thanks God for life, it was fun to live!

I might put it like that.

Why, in short, all these exacting demands? What have we earned? As many boxes of candy as a sweet tooth could desire? Fair enough. But have we not looked on the world each day and heard the soughing of the forest? There is no splendor like the soughing of the forest.

There was a scent of jasmine in a grove, and a tremor of joy ran through one I know, not for the jasmine but for everything—a lit-up window, a memory, the whole of life. But when he was called away from the grove, he had already been paid in advance for this annoyance.

And there it is: the very favor of receiving life at all is handsome advance payment for all life's miseries, each single one.

No, a man should not believe in his right to more candy than he gets. A wanderer advises against all superstition. What is life's? Everything. And what is yours? Is fame? Pray tell us why! A man should not insist on what is "his"; to do so is ludicrous, and a wanderer laughs at anyone so ludicrous. I remember one such who never escaped that "his"; he laid his fire at high noon and finally got it to burn in the evening. Then he couldn't bring himself to leave its warmth for bed, but sat there making the most of it, till others got up again. He was a Norwegian dramatist.

I have wandered around a good deal in my time, and am now grown dull and withered. But I do not hold that perverse graybeard's belief that I am wiser than I was. And I hope, indeed, that I shall never grow wise; it's a sign of decrepitude. If I thank God for life, it is not on the strength of any increased maturity that has come with age but because I have always enjoyed being alive. Age confers no maturity; age confers nothing beyond old age.

I came too late this year to the woods where the berries grow, but I made the journey nonetheless. I have allowed myself this frivolity as a reward for being so capable in the summer. And I reached my goal on the twelfth of December.

It is true, no doubt, that I could have stayed down among the villages. Something would surely have turned up for me, as it has for all those others who have felt it was time for them to settle down. And Lars Falkenberg, my colleague and companion, has advised me to take a clearing, with a wife, two cows, and a pig.

It was a counsel of friendship, the voice of the people. And consider—one of my cows could be a gelded ox for riding, and then I would have transport for the days of my toothless mumbling. But the scheme foundered, it foundered! My wisdom has not come with age; instead, I have come to Trovatn and the moors and forests, and am living in a logger's cabin.

What pleasure can there be in that? Ah, Lars Falkenberg, and ah, all the rest of you—never fear, I have a man who comes here every weekday with a loaf of bread.

So I saunter and saunter in circles around myself, enjoying myself, tasting solitude. I miss Bishop Pavels's seal, which I got from one of his descendants.* I had it in my waistcoat pocket this summer; but when I felt for it just now, I could not find it. Well, well. Still, I have received advance payment for this annoyance in once having owned the ring.

---

* Claus Pavels (1769–1822), Bishop of Bergen, wrote a famous autobiography and kept diaries of which five volumes were published by his grandson. The material published is rated very high, not least for its honesty; and possibly Hamsun's reference to Pavels's seal is a lament that he has become more personally reticent since the days of *Hunger.* In any case, there seems to be some connection between the honesty of the diaries and what Hamsun regarded as the dishonesty of much "literature."—Trans.

Literature, however, I do not miss.

Here am I remembering the twelfth of December and any and every date, while cheerfully forgetting more important things! In the first place, literature: the fact that Captain Falkenberg and his wife had many books in their home—novels and plays, a whole bookcase full. I saw it while painting windows and doors at Øvrebø. They had whole series of authors, and authors' whole series—thirty books. Why the whole series? I don't know. Books—one, two, three, ten, thirty. They had come one each Christmas, novels, thirty volumes—the same novel. Presumably the Captain and his wife read them, always knew what they would find in these Home Library authors—there were pages and pages about everything coming right in the end. Presumably they read them—how should I know? My God, how much literature there was—two men could not shift the bookcase when I needed to paint behind it, three men and a cook were needed to shift it. One of the men was Grindhusen; he turned red under the weight of Home Library authors and said, "I can't understand what people do with all these endless books."

As if Grindhusen understood anything about anything! Presumably the Captain and his wife had all these books so that none should be missing; there they stood, complete. It would make a gap if one of them was removed. They were all alike, all matching: homogenized poetry, the same novel.

There's been an elk hunter with me in the cabin. His visit was no great event; and his dog did nothing but snarl. I was glad when he left. He took down my copper pan from the wall, used it for cooking, and left it all sooted up.

Not that it is my copper pan; it was left in the cabin by someone who'd been here before. I merely took it and scoured it with ashes and hung it on the wall to serve me as a weather prophet. Now I sit polishing it up again, for it's a good thing to have: it goes dim without fail if there's rain or snow in the offing.

It occurs to me that if Ragnhild had been here now, she would have stepped in and polished that copper pan. But on second thought, I would rather look after my weather prophet myself; Ragnhild could find something else to do. And if this place in the woods was our clearing, she would have the children, the cows, and the pig—but as for *my* copper pans, Ragnhild, I intend to take care of those myself!

I remember a married lady who took care of nothing, least of all herself. And ill she fared in the end. But six or seven years ago I could not have imagined anyone so sensitive and lovely toward another human being as she was. I was her coachman on a journey, and she was shy with me, although she was the mistress that I served; she blushed and looked down. And the strange thing is that she made me bashful too, although I was her servant. Just by looking at me with her two eyes when she gave me an order, she showed me beauties and values beyond those I knew already; I remember it still. Yes, I sit here remembering it still, and shaking my head and saying to myself, How strange it was—ah no, no, no! Then she died. What more? Nothing more. I remain. But her death should cause me no sorrow: had I not been paid in advance when she looked at me, undeserving as I was, with her two eyes? Surely that's how it is!

Woman—what do wise men know about woman?

I remember a wiseacre who wrote about woman. He wrote about woman in thirty volumes of homogenized dramatic poetry—I counted the volumes once in a big bookcase. Finally he wrote about the woman who left her own children in search of—the miracle of miracles! What, then, were the children? Oh, it was ludicrous, and a wanderer laughs at anything so ludicrous. *

_____

\* The willfully misleading reference is to Nora Helmer in *A Doll's House*—the first of the great series of prose dramas (of the major

What does the wise man know about woman?

In the first place, he doesn't grow wise until he has grown old, and by then his knowledge of woman is confined to his memory. And, in the second place, he *has* no memory of her, because he has never known her. The man with a talent for wisdom busies himself, miser-fashion, with this talent and with nothing else, tending it and nursing it, displaying it and living for it. One doesn't go to woman for wisdom. The four wisest heads in the world, who have delivered their opinions on woman, simply sat and dreamed her up themselves; they were dotards, young or old, who rode their gelded oxen. They knew nothing of woman in her sanctity, woman in her sweetness, woman as a vital necessity; but they wrote and wrote about woman. Just think, without ever meeting her!

God preserve me from growing wise! Yes, I intend to mumble toothlessly to my deathbed bystanders: God preserve me from growing wise!

---

work only *Brand* and *Peer Gynt* are in verse) which Ibsen wrote in his fifties and sixties; this late flowering explains the slighting reference, on p. 244, to an unnamed "Norwegian dramatist." In 1890 Hamsun had attacked Ibsen to his face in a notorious public lecture.— Trans.

It's a pleasantly cool day for an excursion I've had in mind; the snow peaks are rosy in the sun and my copper pan points to fair. The hour is eight in the morning.

Knapsack, a good supply of food, some spare cord in my pocket, should anything break; money on the table, in case the man comes with a loaf for me while I'm away.

Oh yes, I've been giving myself great airs for my own benefit: I was going on a long journey, I must make meticulous preparations, I would need all my resourcefulness and powers of endurance. Yes, the man who is going on a long journey may give himself such airs; but they hardly match my case. I have no mission, no places I must visit; I am just a wanderer setting out from a logger's cabin and coming back to it again; it makes no difference where I am.

The woods are peaceful and deserted; everything stands there in the snow, holding its breath as I pass. At noon I see from a hilltop Trovatn far behind me; the lake lies there, white and flat, six miles of chalk in the snowy wilderness. After lunch I go on again, I climb higher and higher, I approach the real mountains, but slowly and reflectively, with my hands in my pockets. There is no hurry—I only need to find a spot where I can take shelter for the night. Around three o'clock I sit down and eat a bit more, as though I needed food and had earned it. But it is only for something to do; my hands are idle, and my brain inclined to fancies. It gets dark early; good, here is a snug cleft in the mountainside, with plenty of wind-felled firs to make a fire.

Such are the things I tell of now, playing on muted strings.

I am out early next morning, as soon as the sky lightens a little. Snow begins to fall, soft and warm; there is a soughing in the air. Bad weather brewing, it seems—who would have guessed it? Neither I nor my weather prophet, twenty-four hours ago. I leave my shelter and continue over moors and marshes. Noon comes around again, and it is snowing. My shelter last night was none too good: I had plenty of pine needles for my couch and I didn't get cold, but the smoke from my fire blew all over me and interfered with my breathing.

But this afternoon I find a better place, an extensive, elegant cave, with walls and a roof. There is room both for me and my fire, and the smoke rises vertically. Here I nod and put down my things, although it is early still and broad daylight. I can distinctly make out hills and valleys and rocks leading up to a bare mountain straight ahead, several hours' walk away. But I nod as if I have arrived, and start laying in firewood and pine needles for the night.

How completely I feel at home here! It was not for

nothing that I nodded and put down my things. "Was this your destination?" I ask myself as a joke. "Yes," I answer.

The soughing in the air has grown stronger; the snow has turned to rain. It is strange: heavy, wet rain is running down over the cave and soaking the trees outside; yet it is the cold Christmas month, it is December. A heat wave has contrived to visit us.

During the night it rains and rains, and the soughing continues in the forest outside, as if it were spring. Finally it fills my slumber with a pleasure so profound that I sleep a good sound sleep until far into the day.

It is ten o'clock.

The rain has ceased, but it is still warm. I sit looking out of my cave and listening to the forest as it bends and soughs. Then a stone in the mountainside opposite breaks loose and butts against a rock, which in turn breaks loose; thuds are heard in the distance. Then it turns to a roar, which echoes through me, and I see what is happening: the rock has loosened other rocks, it is an avalanche, stones and snow and earth go thundering down the mountainside, a swirl of smoke rises in the wake of the mighty train. The stream of granite boulders looks positively brutish—thrusting, slashing, teeming, streaming, streaming, filling up a chasm in the valley—and stopping. The last stones sink slowly to rest, and all is over; the thunder out there is silenced, and only my breathing resembles a slowly descending bass.

And now I sit once more and listen to the soughing of the forest. Is it the distant Aegean I can hear, or the ocean current Glimma? I grow weak from sitting and listening, memories well up within me from my life: a thousand joys, music and eyes and flowers. There is no splendor like the soughing of the forest, it is like rocking, it is like madness: Uganda, Antananarivo, Honolulu, Atacama, Venezuela…

But it must be my years that make me so weak, my nerves that join in the sounds I hear. I get up and stand by the fire to calm myself; for that matter, I could talk to the flame a little, make a speech while the fire dies. I am standing in a fireproof house, with good acoustics. Hm.

Then a shadow falls over the cave, and there is the elk hunter again, with his dog…

It is starting to freeze as I wander back home to my logger's cabin; soon the frost bites into moors and marshes, and makes the going easy. I saunter onward, slowly and indifferently, with my hands in my pockets. Why should I hurry? It makes no difference where I am.

GREEN INTEGER
Pataphysics and Pedantry

*Edited by Per Bregne*
Douglas Messerli, *Publisher*

Essays, Manifestos, Statements, Speeches, Maxims,
Epistles, Diaristic Notes, Narratives, Natural Histories,
Poems, Plays, Performances, Ramblings, Revelations
and all such ephemera as may appear necessary
to bring society into a slight tremolo of confusion
and fright at least.

*

Green Integer Books

*Rectification of Eros* Sam Eisenstein [2000]
*Drifting* Dominic Cheung [2000]
*Victoria* Knut Hamsun [2001]


Green Integer EL-E-PHANT books:

*The PIP Anthology of World Poetry of the 20th Century,*
*Volume 1*
Douglas Messerli, editor [2000]
*readiness / enough / depends / on* Larry Eigner [2000]


## BOOKS IN PREPARATION

*Operatics* Michel Leiris
*The Doll* and *The Doll at Play* Hans Bellmer
[with poetry by Paul Éluard]
*Suicide Circus: Selected Poems*
Alexei Kruchenykh
*American Notes* Charles Dickens
*Prefaces and Essays on Poetry*
William Wordsworth
*Confessions of an English Opium-Eater*
Thomas De Quincey
*The Renaissance* Walter Pater
*Venusburg* Anthony Powell
*Captain Nemo's Library* Per Olav Enquist
*Against Nature* J. K. Huysmans
*Partial Portraits* Henry James
*Utah* Toby Olson